Joseph Cox's

The Assessors

And other Torah Stories

Volume 3:
Leviticus - ויקרא

Joseph J. Cox

Published by Big Picture Books

Modiin, Israel

Cover Photography from Shutterstock

Edited by Wouter Dreyer

Feedback from many friends & associates – you know who you are!

Dedicated to the community at:
Lechu Neranena Modiin

Without their encouragement and support
this book would not have been possible

Contents

Introduction

The idea of using stories to explain moral concepts is probably as old as human vocabulary itself. Stories, not rules or arguments, have generational impact, transferring values from one generation to the next. They establish and explain the core character of the societies that carry them. Because of this power, stories have long been used to explain concepts in the Torah.

However, to modern ears many such stories are foreign; either their concepts are unfamiliar, or their styles fail to grip the modern conscious.

This book provides a new set of modern, relatable and engaging stories. They cross many genres and are meant to engage many different kinds of people. I know that writing them has left me with a far stronger understanding of the Torah, of humanity and of the world that surrounds us.

Perhaps you, the reader, can find that same understanding. And, perhaps, these stories will also strengthen your relationship to G-d and your understanding of our place in the world.

Thank you,

Joseph Cox

Book of Vayikra: Sailor

The following story focuses on themes that run throughout the book of Vayikra (Leviticus).

"Can he know?" My grandfather's voice is almost quavering as he asks this simple question. I have never seen him worried about anything. I have no idea what he's worried about now. I look to the powerfully built men, Pacific Islanders, who are regarding my grandfather with careful consideration. Maybe they have an answer.

And then one of them, some sort of chieftain, just nods.

"Yes," he says. In English. It is the first word I've heard him speak.

My grandfather lets out his breath in a whoosh. I still have no idea what is going on.

Perhaps, if I figure it out, my life will begin to make sense.

Surely, you've heard of old money. Well, my family has *very* old money. The nouveau riche exhibits the fear and desperation of quickly made money. They feel a need to share and display their success. But old money is different. It just *is*. But most 'old money' families have had their fortunes for a century, at most. Our family is different. We've had it for hundreds of years.

Which is what made my upbringing so odd. After all, if you were entrusted with that kind of fortune, you'd expect some kind of indoctrination into the family business or the family values. You'd expect to be taught, at least, to manage some massive stable of assets. You'd expect some kind of exposure.

But my family did none of that. I didn't even know that was odd.

I was nine when I realized all the other kids in my private school seemed to know something about their families' money. This one was in banking. That one in real estate. The other in commodities. They asked me what my family did, but I had no idea. All I knew was that my family's fortune was far older than any of theirs. I just thought the actual nature of a family's money was the kind of thing people didn't discuss. Somehow, I thought it wasn't polite.

Perhaps I would have been right if I'd lived in another time.

That day, I asked my parents what they knew. I wanted to tell my friends. Even *they* knew nothing. Sure, they regularly jetted off to exotic locations to spend some time in the family's various homes. But they had no idea where their money came from. I tried researching the source of the money online, but I found nothing. Everything seemed hidden.

Eventually, with growing dread, I gave in to asking the only person who might really know.

My grandfather.

Unlike my father, my grandfather was a huge, imposing and austere man. He wore a full beard and had eyes that seemed constantly disappointed in his family. I was afraid of him. I was afraid of how he'd react. But I mustered the courage and walked up to him – that same day – and I asked him where our family got our money.

He looked down at me, and I saw the faint glimmering of a smile. And then he said the last thing I expected him to say: "It's about time you learned how to cook."

What followed can hardly be believed. My grandfather pulled me from school. He announced, with no resistance from my parents, that from that point onwards I would learn what I needed at home. And then, he began to teach me to *cook*. Day after day, week after week and then year after year, we spent hours cooking. We cooked in the kitchen, we cooked over barbeques, and we cooked over open fires.

And we moved beyond food preparation itself. I learned how to butcher meat and I learned how to prepare a table. I learned how to wait on others. I learned service. And his disapproving eyes watched me every step of the way.

All of it just confused me.

There were no chefs in the family; I had never even seen my grandfather cook. How could this possibly be this important? And how could he possibly know so much?

But I kept cooking. Gradually my confusion was replaced by a desire for praise. I was pouring myself into the food. Then, one night, I remember waiting tableside while my grandfather sampled my latest dish. I stood there, and then I realized that I wasn't waiting for a word of praise. I was waiting to see his joy. And, somehow, he knew it. He turned his face up to me and his always disappointed expression vanished. For the very first time, I saw the face of true satisfaction and open-ended kindness.

Then he said, "I think you're ready."

We took a trip then. Not to Switzerland or the Bahamas. Instead, my grandfather packed a bag full of spices and we flew to Jakarta. My grandfather handed me a passport with a name I'd never seen before, and we declared our spices at customs. In Indonesia, the import of drugs carries the death penalty. It was best to avoid confusion. Then we then took another plane to a smaller island. There, we left our phones and computers in a locker. Finally, we took a boat to yet another island where we ended up at a busy market. We were the only white people on an island of locals speaking a language I couldn't begin to understand. We weren't there long, though. In the market, a huge man saw us. Without a word, he gestured for us to follow him, and we did. He brought us to a small shack, patted us down and then ran some sort of a scanner over us.

Not a word was spoken.

Finally, he gestured us out to a boat. We sailed away from the island. As we were sailing, he unfurled a canopy the color of the sea. It covered the entire boat. We were made invisible, a tiny boat on a massive sea, free of any electronic devices.

We sailed for three days. I have no idea where we went; I knew nothing about navigation. Eventually, as dusk on the third day approached, our little boat ran up on a sandy beach. It was dark and a little chilly. Waiting before me was a circle of powerful and muscled Pacific-Islander men. They were wearing red waistclothes and simple white headdresses, armbands and anklets.

Otherwise, they were completely naked.

They looked me over. Then they nodded to my grandfather, and he handed me a small slip of paper. I unfolded it and saw a recipe. And then a goat was shoved towards me.

I knew what I had to do. I slaughtered and butchered the goat, I prepared the fire, I prepared the meat and the spices, and I began to cook. Two exhausting hours later, I served the meal. I don't know why, but I hoped these men would enjoy it. I hoped that it would please them.

As they licked their fingers, my grandfather asked his question: "Can he know?"

It was then that they agreed.

The man who seems to be the chief reaches behind him and pulls out an ancient-looking diary.

"Read," he says, simply.

I do.

The language is English, but the book is old, and the spelling is unfamiliar. I slowly begin to crawl through it, as the men patiently watch. As I move through it, I realize the book is the diary of a sailor.

He was from England. His mother had been a cook in a big house. But he wanted more and so he signed up to be a sailor on a spice-trading ship. The diary had all the normal accounts of a lowly sailor on a 17th century trading ship. It told of the drudgery and difficulties of that life. Everything was as you'd expect.

And then, suddenly, the story took a turn. The sailor's ship was beached in a violent storm on some unknown island. The natives who lived there slaughtered his crew and the diarist soon discovered he was the sole survivor.

Then, as he watched, the natives started a barbeque. The man feared the natives were cannibals. He thought they would cook the crew. But his desire to survive trumped all else. And so, he offered to help with the cooking. The ship was full of spices, and he knew how to use them. Thankfully, they agreed.

He was doubly thankful that they wanted him to cook goats – not the crew. The sailor did such a good job that they let him live. But only for a day. He recorded the recipe as if it would be his last, a recipe that had saved his life.

I recognized it, it was what I had just prepared.

The next day, he came up with another recipe and then another and then another. And as time passed, he learned their language. He talked to them, and he discovered that they killed his crew because they feared them. Something, on another island, had gone terribly wrong.

Bit by bit, the sailor started cooking not to survive, but to seek the praise of his captors. Eventually, he realized he just wanted to satisfy them. He was truly their servant.

And that was when they showed him their secret.

Deep in a cave in the center of the island was a stunning collection of pearls. The islanders gathered the pearls from a spot off the coast. They were not the only ones to do so. On another island, close by, there had been other pearl collectors. Those islanders had tried to sell their pearls to passing merchants. But the merchants slaughtered the natives and took what they desired.

That was why the crew had been killed; these natives feared the same outcome.

They had killed until they were sure the sailors were no threat.

The sailor asked why the natives were showing him the pearls. They told him: His service to them, through his cooking, had shown that he could be trusted. Most critically, they needed an agent to sell their pearls.

The sailor ended the diary then. Closing the book on one chapter in his life.

"What happened next?" I ask, fearing the man had died.

"Our ancestor," my grandfather says, "took a small boat to sea. He took a stash of pearls with him. They were sewn into his threadbare clothes. He sailed until he came to another island, one with Europeans. He arrived hungry and desperate. But he told nobody where he had been. All he did was sell a few pearls, pearls he claimed to have found. And with the money he earned, he bought himself passage back to England. There, he unstitched his clothes and sold off his great fortune. He went from being a poor sailor and the son of a cook to being a wealthy man. And he sunk everything into his own ship. He then plied the seas, trading for spices. But every few years he would travel, with a small and trusted crew, to that island. To *this* island. He would share the newest recipes and finest spices with the natives. When even his trusted crew wasn't watching, he would be given a collection of the world's most beautiful pearls."

I just look at him, expecting this all to be some elaborate joke.

He simply continues, as serious as ever. "Our ancestor showed his service through his food. The islanders grew to trust him. We return here, whenever we think one of us is worthy. Your father would not have passed. Only those who might cook for the islanders and thus show dedication and a sense of service. We make that very first recipe. And if these islanders accept us, our relationship continues."

"Spices for pearls?" I ask.

"Not anymore," says my grandfather. "These islanders are fantastically rich. They live in other places and have cash deposited in offshore accounts. But they come here to harvest their crops – which we then sell. We maintain their anonymity and thus the secrecy of this place. It is still a very secret place. They also come here, roughly once in a half century, to determine whether any of us are worthy of continuing the relationship. They know that if we come to serve, if we prepare our meal with true dedication, that they can trust us. It is how they grew to trust the sailor in the diary."

"And if they trust us," he concludes, "Then all of us can benefit from an ancient and profitable exchange."

The muscular islander looks at me, a menacing gleam in his eye. "It must all remain secret," he says.

I nod, seriously.

"Remember," the giant man continues, "The goat was cooked well, but the recipe could work on you as well."

I swallow, hard, but I understand.

Our family has been sustained on service and trust.

And it is only service and trust that will carry us into the future.

With that in mind, I look to the chief and ask, "Can you stay for another meal?"

The Book of Vayikra (Leviticus) is focused on the symbolism of a holy people and their priests. It opens with the idea of animal offerings. With an offering, a physical, living, animal is made into something else. It is used to strengthen the spiritual connection between G-d and the Jewish people.

The story above shows an animal used in the same way. It is a goat, slaughtered and cooked, which solidifies the relationship between these peoples. It is the goat that preserves their history and carries them into the future. And it is a goat that is a stand-in for the descendants of the sailor who kept the diary.

The concept of animal sacrifice might seem strange to us now. It is not so unfamiliar, though. Ideally, the animals we eat are not simply protein and calories consumed while we drive to work. Ideally, the meals in which we consume animals help to form the bonds between us, strengthening our families and societies.

In this light, animal sacrifices are not so strange. Instead of being acts of destruction, they are acts of sanctification. They are acts of service in which our relationship to G-d is reinforced and our ability to serve as her agents in this world is carried forward to another generation. They are acts which bring people together and serve as a conduit to blessing.

We no longer offer animal sacrifices. Nonetheless, the concept remains. Through service and dedication, we can build a relationship with G-d.

Through service and dedication, we can be blessed by him.

And through service and dedication, we can fulfill our purpose as a people.

Vayikra: Peace

The following is adapted from my book, the City on the Heights. It is set in northern Iraq, where Maryam has fled with her brother Ibrahim who has suffered some sort of head injury.

The empty village on the border of the mountainous regions of Kurdistan had only twelve houses. Tiny shards of those mountains seemed to thrust out of the landscape, while deep wadis sliced through it, created by the seasonal waters that rushed down to the nearby river. The fields themselves were shaped within this landscape —formed fit to whatever flat terrain could be found between the shards and the crevices. There were no right angles. The houses themselves followed no clear pattern. They looked like they had been placed like children's blocks, scattered almost randomly at the center of the farms themselves. The two features of the village, the fields and houses, seemed to compete with one another in their apparent randomness.

This land was not important or valuable. It was so marginal that some who lived on it were forced to spend their winters in the warmer climates downriver; the harvests weren't substantial enough to support them year-round. But this was not wintertime, and the partially harvested wheat and the leftover food spoke to the urgency of their flight.

It felt odd to seek refuge in a place they had sought refuge from.

But there was no better place for us to go.

The fields weren't large, but for two orphans, they could be an almost endless resource. So long as we could harvest it.

I set off in search of equipment and before long I came to a large shed. Opening it, I found what we would need. There was no combine there, of course. Nearer to Mosul, it was combines that dominated the harvest. A single machine would cut the wheat, beat the grains off the sheaves and then separate the grains from the chaff. But not here. The fields weren't large or square or rich enough. Instead, laying in a tool shed, we found scythes. They had long blades at sharp angles to the sticks that held them. You would hold and sweep the sticks in broad motions and the blades at the bottom – parallel to the ground – would mow the grain. These tools would not make the job easy, but they would enable us to rescue this harvest. We could collect the grain and leave it for them, in safekeeping. We'd eat some, of course. But we'd leave the villagers better off for having granted us their unwilling hospitality.

I chose a scythe and we headed into the fields. There were no child sizes for my brother, Ibrahim.

When I came to the first of the crops, I extended the scythe and pulled it along the bottoms of the first rank of the wheat. Some of it fell, but I was stopped long before I'd completed a full sweep. It required an enormous amount of force to pull the scythe through the grain – far more than I'd imagined.

I brought the scythe back and tried again, pulling harder. I almost made a complete sweep before being brought to a reluctant stop. I tested the blade, it was sharp. This was just incredibly difficult work.

So, I made another sweep and finally brought down the first row of the stalks.

I called my brother over and we used some of the grain to tie the rest. It was our very first sheave.

As I worked, I showed my brother what to do, and he seemed to be following. That's why I was surprised when I made another sweep and he just stood there, watching.

"Gather it up," I said.

He looked at me, pleasantly, and said, "How?"

He had always been a kid who could concentrate. He could always remember. He would remember conversations over months. And yet here he was, forgetting something as simple as tying grain.

"You know how," I said, "I just showed you."

He looked at me blankly. Then he said, "What?"

I surprised myself when I shouted, "JUST DO IT!"

I felt like he was being intentionally slow.

But when he looked at me blankly, and then he started to cry, I finally knew that something was fundamentally wrong.

I calmed myself and showed him how to gather the grain. Then, I scythed another row of the grain. And then, I showed him how to gather again. I realized I was doing both jobs, but I hoped, somehow, that he'd learn what he needed to learn. I kept scything, pushing myself as hard as I physically could. My progress was slow. I was harvesting grain, but I was also fighting, helplessly, against whatever was wrong with my wounded brother. The work was hard, and I removed my niqab from on top of my cotton pants and shirt. There were no men nearby.

We took a break in the early afternoon. We went down to the river and filled our water bottles – then chlorinated and drank. I had found some sesame flour that morning, and I mixed it into a paste. We ate it. It wasn't pleasant, but it was nutritious.

And then we got back to work.

It became almost routine. I would cut, putting all of my meager force into the action. Then I would stop and help Ibrahim gather and tie the grain. We repeated it, again and again. By the end of the day, we had covered an area of 100 feet by 5 feet. The rest of fields, which had looked so manageable earlier in the day, now seemed overwhelming. But we had made progress. We had harvested something. In the place of the even field, there were now little towers made up of the sheaves we had cut and tied.

We slept for the night. In the morning, I decided to try my hand at baking. My mother had never really taught me how to cook. I mixed some of the flour in one of the houses with water and kneaded it as I imagined it ought to be done. Then I baked it in a charcoal-powered stove. The result was somehow both lumpy and flat. But it was food. The effort of baking had taken all morning. In the afternoon, my tired muscles didn't feel like scything – it seemed like every thrust demanded all the energy I had at that moment. And each pass needed to be followed by another. I'd never done anything so exhausting.

Luckily, there were other things to do, so we headed for the fields once again. This time we were in search of sheaves for threshing.

...

There was a threshing machine in the far rear of the shed. It was small – and in place of a gas engine on the side, it had a single pedal at its front. It looked like it hadn't been used in a dozen years.

We wheeled it out of the shed, together. I found oil and some tools and set to fixing the old contraption up. This machine's mechanical elements were obvious. The rollers would thrash the grain together, a manual fan would gently blow away the chaff, and the grain itself would fall through a grate in the bottom. All of it would be driven by the pedals.

It was already near the end of the day when I had the machine running smoothly. I would push the pedal, and everything would move in unison, and then as the crush-blow-collection cycle was completed, the pedal would rise to be pushed down again. The motion was almost like biking, one-legged.

I stood in front of the machine, pushed the pedal, and lay the dry grain against the top of the machine. It worked beautifully and quietly. The grains were ripped off the ends of the stalks. The chaff blew out the back of the machine in a gentle cloud and – almost like mechanical magic – the grain itself emerged out of the chute. It was perfect.

Over the next week, we alternated harvesting and gathering dry grain for threshing. My legs, torso and arms began to ripple with newfound strength. It felt both exhausted and physically exhilarated. Sometimes, I could even complete entire sweeps of the scythe in a single pass. Best of all, Ibrahim learned. He learned to gather the fallen stalks and tie them by himself. He figured out how to help me carry them. And he learned how to lay the grains against the rotors of the machine as they were thrashed. He couldn't plan – multiple steps were beyond him. But, with enough practice, he could repeat.

We were steadily consuming the village's meager food stocks. While I wanted to keep harvesting, we did need to eat. We needed to make flour out of the grain. This challenge was very different from extracting the grain itself. While farms like these would have equipment for threshing and winnowing, grinding was another matter. Grinding was an industrial process. There were only a few silos in the entire region. Farmers would sell their grain to the central government – at inflated prices – and the government would grind it into flour and sell it onwards at a lower market rate. This overpayment for grain was one way in which Baghdad kept its influence in the north. But given the price of that grain – and the attention given to the subsidies behind that price – I couldn't imagine individual farmers would keep much of their produce for themselves. It wouldn't have made any sense for them to do their own grinding. My exploration of the kitchens bore that out. We had used flour, but it had all come in bags with the flag proudly displayed on it. The farmers had sold the grain at inflated prices and then bought back the flour at a cheaper price.

Of course, the central government hadn't always subsidized the farms in this way. I thought that there must be some equipment left from an earlier era – just as the manual thresher had been. I dug through the shed, and then house after house, looking for something to grind the grain with. I needed, somehow, to make flour.

Finally, I found something that might work. It was a small hand mill. It had two stone rollers, both of which were connected to a single wheel with a crank. A hopper rose above them. Crank the wheel, and the stone rollers would rub against each other. Pour grain into the hopper, and it would fall to the point at which the rollers met. Keep cranking the wheel, and the grain would be pulled between the rollers, crushed and transformed into flour. The remarkable thing about the small device – after so much searching – was that it was in plain sight. It was mounted on a wall in the kitchen area of one of the small village houses. It was in excellent condition and hadn't been used that long ago; only a small patina of dust had gathered on its surfaces. I wondered why it had been in use, before the villagers had fled. Then I smelled it and I understood. It smelled of sesame. The people who lived here used it to make sesame flour from seeds. It was never intended for wheat.

I was worried it wouldn't work, but I had few other options. To my delight, it functioned perfectly. So, Ibrahim and I brought some grain to the kitchen, and we ground it. Like every other part of the process, it was hard work. Rather than working my legs or my torso, it worked my arms. Around and around, they went, pulling the crank and grinding the flour. After an hour – and after seeing the rough quality of the result – I understood why this was an industrial process.

But we needed to eat. So, Ibrahim slowly poured the grain into the hopper, and I ground the wheel. Around and around.

As the grain flowed out the side of the small mill, a sudden euphoria came over me. My brother and I had accomplished something tremendous. We had taken grain – standing in the fields.

We had harvested and threshed and winnowed it. And now, we were grinding it into flour. It was our flour. We had produced it.

I wanted to complete that process. So, I baked bread, with our flour. It was coarse, and there were a few tiny rocks in it. But it was edible. And it was ours.

We kept on that way, week after week under the hot sun, harvesting and threshing and, as we needed to, grinding and baking. My body grew strong. I hadn't been sedentary in Mosul, but short bursts of municipal repair were easy in comparison to weeks of manual harvesting. Now, I was far stronger than I ever had been before. And my endurance had also increased exponentially.

As the weeks progressed, I found yeast, and we learned to pick the rocks out from the grain before baking it. And, just as Ibrahim slowly got better at his tasks, I got better at baking the bread itself. We actually began to look forward to our evening meals. We would sit outside and eat, admiring our progress as more and more of the fields were harvested and processed.

We – just the two of us – were accomplishing something remarkably tangible.

I wasn't alone in my happiness. Ibrahim was delighted. He couldn't keep the history of what we'd done straight; he couldn't keep the whole process in his head. But when he saw the gathered stalks or the buckets of grain or small containers of flour – or even the bread emerging from the oven – he glowed with joy. He was accomplishing something – and, somehow, he knew it.

Every morning, Ibrahim would ask about our parents. And every day, I would give him the same answer, "Ibrahim, they aren't here." He always, somehow, seemed satisfied with what I told him. One evening, as we sat there eating our evening meal, I found myself hoping that somehow, our parents could see us. And then I felt that they were. I can't explain it, but I could feel that they were proud.

I turned to my little brother. "Ibrahim," I said, "They're here."

Just that once, just like before the bomb, he knew what conversation I was continuing.

He smiled, joyfully. "Yes," he said, "They are."

Of course, the grain, and even my parents' pride, weren't the only development of those weeks in the village. All-h had answered my prayers as we'd run from Mosul. It was when my brother woke up, on the low hills overlooking Kalak, that the nature of those prayers changed. Before, I had prayed for help – out of desperation. I had prayed out of a kind of greed. I had prayed on my schedule and around my desires. But when he woke up, I began to pray to glorify All-h. I prayed on His schedule, and in the way He and His prophet commanded. I prayed to connect to Him and to bring Him into my life. And I prayed because I was overwhelmed by the responsibility of who I needed to be.

I needed His guidance and the reassurance of His path.

Ibrahim and I had grown up secular. Even after the Americans came, my father seemed to cling to a vestige of Baathist philosophy. But the world of Mosul was a religious one. I couldn't not know the call to prayer, the opening verses of the Koran, and the rituals connected to them. And I couldn't not know the times of prayer. For my entire life, the muezzins' loudspeakers had proclaimed the dominance of Islam in the city. At dawn, sunrise, midday, midafternoon, sunset and nightfall, their voices rang against the walls of every neighborhood – proclaiming the times of prayer and dominating those who were not Muslim. I had never paid much attention to those loudspeakers – like many of the less religious, I learned to sleep through them from a very young age. But now, I would rise at dawn each day and recite the Al-Fatiha, and I would close each night with my head bowed to the floor, and the words "Glory be to my Lord, the most High Most Praiseworthy" on my lips.

As we worked, Ibrahim and I lost track of the days of the week. I didn't know which day was Friday – a day for special prayers. But I knew that the next month was Ramadan. I knew the new moon would herald that month. When the moon dwindled and finally disappeared, we began our holy month.

We would still work each day. And, despite the practice of Ramadan forbidding it, we would drink what we needed – our level of manual labor made that essential. But we would only eat and drink to satisfaction after sunset. We imitated the cycle in the city of Mosul. Mosul would be dormant during the day. But it would come to life at night with families and even neighborhoods sharing in daily feasts. The joy, in those days, was palpable.

Somehow, alone in the village, the cycle seemed even more beautiful to me. We would create the entire day. And then we would use our creations for our own little Ramadan feasts. Although I didn't say the prayers over food (because I didn't know them), the work we poured into those celebratory meals seemed to amplify our understanding of All-h's glory and His peace. Our labor seemed to be invested in something timeless, in something greater than our lives. All-h created for six days and rested on the seventh. In a way, we were imitating His path – the straight path – and we were drawing closer to Him as a result.

We didn't manage to harvest all the grain. By the middle of the month of Ramadan, some of the grain had started rotting after having been left on the stalk too long. We cut it anyway, but left the stalks in the fields. I didn't know what I was supposed to do. I was worried the fallen stalks might block some natural processes, but I guessed that they were more likely to help the land fallow effectively. I never did find out if I was right.

And then, one afternoon, we were done. The work in the fields was complete, the collection of barrels in the storehouse was full of grain – and we had everything we needed to last us through the year. That evening, we both went down to the river and bathed and washed our clothes. They dried quickly in the sun. I felt strong and accomplished and deeply satisfied, and I could see Ibrahim felt the same. I was still Maryam Al-Mosuli – but I had also discovered something beyond that heritage.

The next morning felt luxurious. I woke up for my prayers. But then, I just wandered around the village. For the first time since we'd left Mosul, my brother didn't follow me. He was comfortable in the village, and we weren't working together – not that day. When we'd first come to this place, I'd found a left-behind book in one of the houses. I hadn't opened it before, but I did now. I had time to read. It was a children's book: the tales of Ali Baba. The fantastic old stories didn't fill me with as much excitement as they once had. Somehow, though, I could better understand them. In my own way, I had embarked on a dangerous journey, and All-h had rewarded me with great riches.

In the mid-afternoon, I laid out my prayer rug for the Zuhr prayer. I recited the opening verses. I touched my forehead to the prayer rug. And I breathed deeply. I thought of my brother, and I thought of my parents, and I thought of how much we had accomplished. I prayed for All-h's mercy and His forgiveness for my faults and shortcomings. And then I uttered the verse:

Glory be to my Lord, the Most High Most Praiseworthy.

I kept my head bowed to the ground, intent on my joy in the service of All-h.

Then, in the distance, I heard engines.

Fear ripped through me.

And then, in a sudden panic, I realized that I didn't know where Ibrahim had gone.

I wrote this chapter thinking of the Torah reading of VAYIKRA. In VAYIKRA, we learn of the cycle of offerings. We bring offerings to Hashem. But they are not simply things we acquire; they are things we have had a hand in creating. We do not bring fruit or wild animals, but only domesticated animals and the product of our labor. We do not bring bread, which has been leavened by bacteria, except on SHAVUOT. This cycle, or creation and dedication, plays such a critical role in the cycle of Divine fulfillment.

Jews work for six days and rest on the seventh, using the product of our efforts to connect with G-d. To me, Maryam's experience captures this sort of fundamental connection to G-d.

While not directly tied to this story, the concepts behind the offerings are also important. The following reviews those concepts, in a lightly humorous way.

For the purpose of this exercise, the *Shechina* (the resting spirit of G-d) is going to be feminine. It helps that the *Shechina* is *literally* a feminine word. Also, we're also going to adopt some very old-fashioned ideas of courtship for this exercise. We're talking Shang Dynasty era – and I'd never even heard of them before I wrote this sentence. I could explain the antique gender roles, but it is probably more fun just to let you read them and hate me instead for my typecasting.

The first offering we can bring is the *Olah* offering.

It is a willful offering – expressing a simple desire to *give* something of yourself to Miss Shechina. The most famous *Olah* offering of all was Yitzchak. We all know Avraham was expressing Fear of G-d and all that. But that was at the end. Earlier on, he had actually decided to *give something of himself* to G-d. That's the whole point of child sacrifice. Avraham made the decision to do it. It was a willful decision.

The best example my friend could come up with was when he wanted to give something to this woman he'd started dating (turns out, it was his future wife, some gal named Rebecca). He went to a store, we'll call it 'Handley Rock and Jewelry Supply' and looked through all the various types of stones they had. He ended up picking something he thought she'd like. A nice blue rock – a color he liked – and he had it set on a *thin* gold chain, cause he was on a budget after all. But it still represented his own effort and will – some expression of what he was capable of. Sure, it was his brother's idea, but we don't have to get into that. Anyway, that was kind of an *Olah* offering. Except instead of burning it in a dedication to the spiritual world, he stuck it a USPS package and mailed it to Australia.

The *Olah* represents *will* as well as a simple gift. And we can see it in the offerings. They are male. In the Chumash, the male represents the willful while the female represents the actualizing. I can't just let that sit there and have you glower or stop reading because of how... 'Shang Dynasty' I am. In reproductive terms, the male has to decide to contribute. But that decision doesn't yield children. The woman has to actually produce them, although she lacks inherent will in the matter (with birth control and abortion, there is negative will but that's another story). *Adam* plants, *Adama* (the feminine of Adam, which means earth), yields crops. That's the theme. And I'm sorry it it's offensive. I didn't write this stuff.

So, the *Olah* has to be male. And in the case of the little birdy – where it can be very hard to distinguish male and female (so hard that even today they sometimes do genetic tests to work it out) – the potentially 'feminine' aspects are ripped out. The entrails and the crop – which produces milk. Fun fact, the only bird we bring is a dove. Why? It is the only kosher bird that produces milk for its young. It not only nurtures, it is physically *designed* to nurture and support the next generation. We don't just give of ourselves; we bring the *best* of ourselves.

Anyway, we bring this male offering to the *Mishkan* (Tabernacle), we burn it up, and the *Shechina* actualizes our will into spiritual energy – a connection to G-d. Think of it as a USPS package with a blue necklace for Hashem.

The next offering? The *Mincha* offering. And no, it doesn't involve stopping the car on the way home for 10 minutes of prayer on the side of the road. My friend's perfect example of a *Mincha* offering was a book. You see, his potential mother-in-law, who lived in Australia, was a huge *Clan of the Cave Bears* fan. My friend's mother happened to be good friends with the author. So, he got his potential mother-in-law an autographed copy of the book. Why? It was quite obnoxious, but he was trying to *influence* his potential mother-in-law. The classic example is Yaakov sending nuts, a few local spices, date honey and the such to 'the man in Egypt.' He's trying to influence a good outcome by sending a special gift. Something that shows real care.

It is important to get a *Mincha* offering right. Hashem wasn't impressed with Cain's fruit. It was fair, *really*. Fruit, in the Torah, are always a gift from G-d. In an effort to butter up G-d, Cain essentially *regifted* G-d's own gift – back to Him (or Her). Talk about a serious faux pas. He should have known better. Just in case *you* don't know better, the Torah specifically tells us we can't give fruit, honey or leavened bread – you know, the things *we* don't actually have a hand in producing.

What *should* you give when you want to butter up G-d? Oddly, it isn't a copy of *Clan of the Cave Bears*. Why do you give if you want to show G-d you tried and you're trying to be fancy and refined and that you are emotionally invested. First, flour – which involves a tremendous amount of labor (or energy nowadays). Second, oil – which involves a lot of purification and refinement. Finally, incense – which conveys emotion. The Kohanim, who are meant to be pass-throughs for the people, don't bring incense. Their emotions aren't supposed to be a part of the game.

If you want to butter *anybody* up, this is a pretty good idea. Refinement, hard work and emotion; all in a gift! Next time you want a promotion, or a better haircut, keep this in mind.

Next up is *Zevach Shlamim*. To me, *Zevach* means transformation. Think *Mizbeach* or even *Zavat Chalav U'dvash* (land of flowing milk and honey). *Shalom* means 'complete'. This offering is a complete transformation. Like, you're all in. An engagement ring, perhaps? Obvious, I know. But there y'go. Actually, for my friend, it wasn't so obvious.

You can't just give a woman you just met a ring. You have to have some feel for your relationship. That's why the first *Zevach Shlamim* is only given after the Torah Reading of *Mishpatim* – we know ourselves; we know the beginnings and the crux of our relationship with G-d. We say "*Naase v'Nishma*" ("We'll do, and we'll hear"). We are committing. We're all in. *Then* we give a *Zevach Shalmim*.

How do my friend do it? He gave his wife-to-be the ring from a bottle of Coke.

Sometimes my friend disappoints me.

We can give lots of things as a *Zevach Shalamim*. Male, female, cows, goats, sheep – whatever. The key point is, we put our hands on the animal's head. We place ourselves in the animal. It is like we're offering *ourselves* up. This is a *big* deal. There are lots of fun details, but I'll pick just one. A goat isn't directly called a *Zevach Shlamim*, even when given as one. Why? Goats are rambunctious. When you decide to represent yourself as a goat and say, "I'm all in", you're being a bit cheeky.

You know, like giving your fiancé the ring from a plastic bottle of Coke.

After you move in together there's a whole new category of gifts. My friend doesn't know anything about this. But apparently, after you have a fight, you can make up and that's good. When you're just dating, that's one thing. But when you're married and committed, that sort of repair can even make the relationship *stronger*. Weird, I know. Well, we have the same thing here. *After* the Mishkan is built, we can bring a *Chatat* offering. A sin offering. A repair for damages done. I suppose flowers might do. In the case of the Mishkan, different parts of the people (or the nation as a whole) are represented by different animals. The offerings are very similar to the *Zevach Shalamim*. Really, you're reaffirming your dedication – despite mistakes made. My friend says he has a friend who says it can be a very nice and touching thing.

Okay. Let's say you, um, fail to disclose you're married while on a business trip. You mislead people. You create a potentially bad situation. We have a perfect example of it in the Torah. Avraham goes to the Pilishtim, doesn't say Sarah is his wife and bad things result. Avimelech actually says "one of my people might have lain with her and you would have brought upon us *Asham*." Either hiding things, or being suckered by hidden things, leads to an *Asham*. My friend's wife had a cool solution to this. See, he doesn't wear a wedding ring. So, his wife bought him a coffee mug with the faces of the whole family on it. Voila, nobody would be confused by his 'status.' *Asham* avoided.

But what if there was an *Asham*? Well, you have to make up for it. Perhaps you could symbolically show how you're giving up your rambunctious self? Goats are rambunctious, but sheep *enable* rambunctiousness. Either one will do. I like to think it depends on whether you are the deceiver or the deceivee. You pick the offering that represents what you did wrong: either you did the deception yourself or you caused somebody else to be deceived.

What's the last set of offerings? A whole bunch of different situations all linked by the offering of a ram. A *fear* offering. A great example though is stealing from the Holy. This is a no good, very bad, thing. This was a bridge too far, even for my friend. But he had a boss once who bought his wife a vacuum cleaner for their 20th anniversary. We all warned him it was a really really stupid thing to do. He even showed us the model. He was so proud. I have no idea if he is still married... or even alive. But if he is, it probably required an offering like this – a fear offering. The thing is, I can't even think of that kind of offering. I mean, what the heck do you do to repair a vacuum cleaner anniversary gift? I guess that's one of the great things about our relationship with Hashem. He gives us (or She gives us) a road out. A symbol. A way of expressing the fact that we really know we screwed up and that we submit to Her will. A ram, reminiscent of the ram offered in place of Yitzchak, is that symbol.

Our relationship with Hashem is so transcendent we can even make up after gifting G-d a heavenly Roomba on Pesach.

Tzav: The Eden Dawn

It started on June 24th, 2073. At first, Dr. Jillian Smith hadn't noticed it. That didn't last long. Global catastrophes had a way of *making* themselves noticed.

Jillian had just celebrated her one hundred and first birthday. She had been born in 1972. While her age might have made her unusual in 1972, it had no such effect in 2073. There were those who were older, and those who were younger. The distinctions between them had largely vanished. She wasn't an *old* woman, just a woman – albeit an unusual one.

Jillian had grown up much like anybody else. She'd come from Rust Belt Ohio and experienced the economic collapse of the late 1970s and the 'paper boom' – such as it was seen in her small town – of the financially leveraged 1980s. Jillian wasn't like her neighbors, though. She was a driven loner. She was pushed to build and create and change everything around her, but she wasn't driven towards social goals. She didn't care much for actual people. She'd studied biology, happily spending her college years largely alone and in a lab.

Like many in the field, nothing of note came from her work in her early career. She expected this. Physicists and mathematicians were like flashes in a pan. They celebrated their great achievements in their 20s and then spent the rest of their lives trying to use their insights, their necessarily simplistic insights (from her perspective), to explain everything else in the world. It was as if they believed that simply knowing about the Big Bang gave them a complete understanding of everything that came afterwards.

Biologists were a different breed. Their world seemed to exist on another level of complexity, relating only to physics like the experience of tasting a perfect chocolate chip cookie related to the flour that went into it. Biologists took their time to understand. What they eventually understood was fundamentally more profound; at least as Jillian saw it.

As a biologist at Ohio State, Jillian had hardly noticed the Internet Revolution; to her it was only a medium for scientific interaction. As Ohio was largely immune to the housing bust of 2008, she'd hardly noticed that as well. And, as a pre-eminent biologist, the strain on student finances that led to the 'education bust' of 2022 hardly bothered her. She lived off grants, not alumni or student loans. She just continued working.

But she was a biologist. It was as a biologist that she contributed to the greatest change of all. Jillian had been one of the few hundred thousand people who drove the unexpected revolution of the late 2020s. It had been called, even as it was happening, the 'Eden Dawn'. It was during the Eden Dawn that the use of cord blood to refresh old cells had been mastered. It was during the Eden Dawn that programmable biological robots capable of micro-targeting biological invaders had been developed. It was during the Eden Dawn that womankind (biology was a female-dominated field) had learned to reset the clock on cellular regeneration. It was during the Eden Dawn that death itself had been conquered. That was not the only change the Dawn had brought. It had not only been a Dawn of Life, but a Dawn of Prosperity. A.I. (Artificial Intelligence) and mechanization had developed to such a point that no creative human effort was required to sustain human life. A person only needs to eat, subject themselves to increasingly painless medical treatment, and live.

A few hundred thousand people contributed to this change. They had been filled with the excitement of it. The world at large, the billions of others, had only been beneficiaries and observers. Their lives changed, of course. Just not in ways that those who changed them had bothered to try to predict.

It had, perhaps, been an error not to do so.

The world had been freed from death. It had been freed from sickness. It was also, after a tumultuous period of economic reorganization, freed from poverty. Then, everything was replaced by one universal feeling: boredom. Boredom was only the *obvious* word for their condition. Right below that feeling was another, more powerful fear: meaninglessness. In this new world, a world without struggle, people sought distraction. They started by immersing themselves in drugs, and then reversed their addictions using newly developing technologies. They continued by celebrating every biological urge. They dressed in every way (or not at all) and challenged every social norm. This was one of the few ways that age was relevant, those who were older were slower to change. People began to say outrageous things in order to experiment with culture itself. Everything else, after all, could be easily reprogrammed by any individual. Culture had more reality – requiring some sort of consensus. That's why they believed there was nothing more fundamental than the formation of that culture. They battled, literally, over tiny slights – trying to draw at whatever scraps of meaning they could find and pull at them. Because *purpose* was the greatest distraction of all. And culture was the closest they could come to purpose. Some even went to war, risking their immortal lives – just to fight for something. Some went on shooting sprees, for the very same reason.

Throughout it all, Jillian Smith hardly noticed. Even as other biologists and programmers dropped out of their fields, seeing no need to continue, she kept working. She saw nothing outside of her work. She just carried on. She created new programming for the bio-robots. She applied biological knowledge to increase the power of A.I. She even developed the cures for addiction. She also dabbled in others' desires, developing new hallucinogens for them to experiment with. She pushed the world forward, but she was not moving with it. She remained in her lab, creating and building and changing.

Then, immortal mankind decided to create a new distraction. They would return to space. They would bring life to other worlds. Everything would be captured on video. Humankind would feel – at least many of them would – like they were contributing to something meaningful. Of course, robots would do almost all the work. But they needed a mind, a pre-eminent biological mind, to lead the effort.

They needed a scientist.

It wasn't long before the perfect envoy was selected: Jillian Smith. There was really nobody else still up for the challenge.

Jillian started her mission on December 15th, 2070. She left behind a world jumbled in confusion. Even she understood how troubled it was. As she saw it, the biological imperatives of evolution had been defeated. In some way, the biological drives that lay at the heart of species, and of cultures, remained – but they had been deprived of their marrow: everything was chaos, and the world was devoid of meaning (Gn 1:2).

There was some interest in her work. Certainly, she was interested. So, she was launched aboard the biggest rockets the world had ever seen, to experiment and understand the possibilities of life in a universe without the protective magnetic and atmospheric blanket the Earth provided.

But a biologist's work is slow. Even if the generations of a species being studied are fast, it takes generations for that species to change. Soon, the world largely forgot about her. They kept sending her rocketloads of supplies, of course. And one poor soul kept conducting monthly Internet-broadcast interviews with her. Despite the interviewer having a manic jumpiness that reminded Jillian of old Japanese TV, it was clear even the host's heart wasn't in it. Neither was Jillian's. She didn't cry for attention. So, people just forgot about her. She was not distracting enough.

But Jillian was distracted. Her work enveloped her. She was a hundred and one years old, and she was, she felt, in what could be called the new prime age for biologists. She was making great progress. She had developed resilient new life-forms based around a new blood, a blood built around molecules of silver, not iron or copper. She had used the powers of evolution to grow and develop them – nudging them towards the properties they would need in this harsh new world. They were simple still, but they had basic circulatory systems. They were also asexual. She wanted to minimize their distractions.

With her successes, she almost totally forgot about the Earth. She was to distract humankind, but humankind had never distracted her.

That is why she hadn't noticed when the sickness struck.

Jillian herself had engineered a virus perfect for implanting genetic updates. It was a human-engineered replacement for generational evolution. A young group of poorly trained tinkerers had begun to use that virus to experiment on themselves. It was the ultimate distraction: self-driven, and self-applied genetic change. They wanted to express their souls more purely through their bodies. It was risky, but that was part of the point. Then, they made a mistake. Well, two actually.

First, they enabled the virus to survive outside the body – at least for a day or two. It made their tinkering easier. They could create genetic experience rooms: walk in, and change, walk out and change again. It was an uncanny experience.

Secondly, and quite by accident, one of them temporarily gave it properties that collapsed the proteins in blood itself.

It didn't take long for this new virus to spread. Within weeks, it formed the basis of a global contagion. Every living species that had a blood supply, even those with copper-based blood like the octopus, was infected. Every single blood-based species died.

But the rockets kept coming because the robots were immune. So, Jillian didn't notice. Then the time came for her regularly scheduled interview. When the manic woman didn't call, Jillian called her. Nobody answered.

When Jillian turned her attention to Earth, she was struck by what she saw.

Within weeks, it had become a world without animals, human or otherwise. Even the robots, sensing a lack of demand for their products, had stopped working.

Jillian was alone. More than this, she knew, given the constraints of space and time (things defined by those now vanished childish physicists) that she would *always* be alone.

She joked for a moment that she wouldn't miss the physicists. After all, she had as much chance of having a conversation with an ear of corn as she had with one of them. Then she realized she had nobody to share the joke with.

She was alone.

Totally alone in the universe.

For the first time in her life, she noticed.

And so, she set about on a new mission. She wanted – no, she needed – to create life on earth. She started by trying to understand what had gone wrong. Before long, it was clear that the virus which had exterminated blood-based life had died with its hosts. The world was safe for blood. She knew she could begin again.

She turned her efforts to her new project. She met with tremendous success. She extended her lifeforms upwards – adding new attributes and capabilities. After only a few decades of work, she had created new animals and new people. They were not human; they were something else. But they were alive – pumping their silver-blood. They were even intelligent, with the highest forms exhibiting problem-solving and linguistic capabilities. She cherished her creatures, loving them as they developed and grew. But as they became more and more advanced, she realized they lacked *something*.

She realized they had no souls.

She had thought, as she neared her 150th birthday, that she was beyond revelation. But it was not so. There was something beyond biology. There was another level that she did not understand. There was a level of reality that, it seemed, only endless years could unlock.

She tried, though. She tried to create 'soul' in her creatures. They spoke to her, wandering in the garden of plenty that was the earth. She supplied their every need, using her fleet of rots to follow them from place to place. But they had no souls.

She divided them into sexes, hoping the resultant tensions would create what she sought. But there was nothing. They still had no souls. They were like biological programs, not rising to the level of truly independent actors.

She was still alone.

And then, in an act of desperation, she kissed one of them. A male. It had been sleeping. She felt *something* then, she felt like *something* had been transferred. Her emotional investment had created something new.

When her creation awoke, she *knew*, although there was no science behind it, that it now had a soul. Somehow, her kiss had given it that mysterious element.

But its newfound spirituality caused a strange reaction. In her presence, in the presence of its creator, it shut down. It just died. It had a sense of spiritual self, spiritual independence that could not survive the presence of its creator. Its own spirit was negated by her overwhelming presence. Its independence vanished. And so, she withdrew. The creatures she gave soul to were more comfortable with her at a distance. They had room to grow as something more than automatons.

At first, nothing more happened. The newly spiritual creatures did not develop themselves. They were not capable of a true relationship. But, when she withdrew some of their bountiful blessings, she watched them create. When they created, she watched them pour their own emotions and desires into something. She watched their own souls develop, as, she realized, hers had.

As the centuries passed, she learned to speak, indirectly, with them. Life itself became their language. They would ritually place their own souls in lower life forms. And then they would sacrifice those to her, conveying gratitude, or fear, or regret, or love. She loved all her creatures, but she understood the beauty of their offerings. The lower life forms had been created to enable the higher life forms to talk with her. It was the greatest realization of their lives. They were not destroyed by relating to her. Instead, they became part of a new spiritual reality – a matrix connecting creator and created.

She found, when the highest life-forms – the life forms blessed with souls – died, she remained aware of their souls. She could sense that intangible reality. But those souls were not the same ones she had gifted. They had taken what she had given them, and they had developed it. They had colored their souls with the lessons of their lives. Those souls, even in their static, lifeless, incorporeal forms, were beautiful – more beautiful than anything she had encountered before.

She collected them, those souls. She challenged her life forms, using her power to shape their reality and thus help them beautify their own souls.

She used reality to build up that which survived past their mortal existence.

As she worked, collecting souls, her understanding deepened. She knew now that there were levels to all things. Just as the flour was to the experience of a cookie, her biology was to something far greater. Just as the flour might not understand its greater purpose, so too a sacrifice – or a life hard-lived – might not understand how much it had achieved. It achieved, nonetheless.

She lived then, for a time, as a god on earth.

But as her creatures built cultures and societies and networks of interaction, she came to realize her work was done.

Her work was done, but her life was incomplete.

She too had a living soul. And that soul had been gifted to her by another.

That is why, at 969 years of age, the age of Metuselach, she left the earth once again. She rose up into space, aboard another rocket.

But she took no supplies: no water and no food.

As she watched the world below her flourishing once again, she allowed herself to die.

She allowed her soul to be collected by a still greater being. She allowed herself to be forever enmeshed in a greater reality.

And she understood, as so few do, that there was no waste in her death. There was only beauty in what would remain with the truly eternal.

I wrote this for the Torah reading of *TZAV* because of the change in holiness. In *VAYIKRA*, only the bread eaten by the *KOHEN* (priest) is called Holy or Holy of Holies. It is a Torah reading written for the lay person – who sees loss in animal death and even in the burning of flour. But *TZAV* is written for the perspective of the *KOHANIM* (priests), and so many things – the same things – are called Holy. Holiness is objective, from the Divine perspective. However, it is subjective from ours. It is a layer we need not understand. Like Moshe (Moses), we can resist G-d's plans – we can see loss where He sees only greatness. Like a farmer, we can resist the offerings – seeing only the waste of an animal life where He sees the unlocking of the greatest potential. Our lack of vision does not stop us from being embraced by G-d. Quite the contrary, that lack of vision can be key to the development of our souls.

Shemini: A Child's Terror

The boy looks up at me. I am always struck by his incredibly intense eyes. But there is fear in those eyes now, a deep and troubling fear.

"Grandma?" he asks, his breath splitting the chilly night air.

"Yes," I answer, my voice shaking.

"Is G-d going to kill me too?"

I don't know the answer to his question. How could I? How can I understand what has happened?

I stroke the boy's hair gently.

"No," I say, calmly, "G-d won't kill you."

I've said it, but I'm not sure I believe it. He looks at me, doubtfully. It is time to sleep, but he will be consumed by nightmares. How could he not? *I* will be consumed by nightmares, and I am not a child.

One minute, Nadav and Avihu had been approaching the MISHKAN (Tabernacle) our people had built. The next minute, they had been consumed by a heavenly fire.

It had happened only hours ago.

The entire community is still in shock, and I know I'm not the only woman trying to calm a frightened child.

And what had Moshe (Moses), our great leader, done? He'd tried to make Aaron act as if nothing had happened. But *something* had happened.

When Aaron made it clear that he was in no state to celebrate, Moshe had accepted that. But *then* he'd gone on one of his law-giving binges. He'd gone on and on about what kinds of animals and birds and fish we can or can't eat.

I'm sure the man is holy, but he has no sense for people.

The little boy is still looking at me. He's only five, but he's seen so much already. These last few years have been both miraculous and frightening.

I need to give him something to hold on to. But I don't know what. Then I have an idea.

"Can you see the string?" I ask.

"What string?" the boy replies.

"The string," I say, "That connects us."

He looks at me, very seriously, and says, "There is no string, grandma."

"Of course there is," I say, "I am connected to you. And you are connected to me. It's a string that connects us. You can't see it, but it is even more real than my hand or your nose."

His eyes widen. I keep going. "We have strings that go all over the place. Some are thick and strong, like our string. But others are thin and weak."

He's listening, carefully.

"But one string is the most important, and hardest of all to see. Do you know which string that is?"

He shakes his head, no.

"The string from us to Hashem," I say. "That string is called holiness. And it crosses from our world – where there are physical things and where things change – to His world – where everything is spiritual and where nothing changes."

"Moshe said Nadav and Avihu strengthened that string," the boy whispered, "He said their death sanctified G-d. How can that be?"

I'm stunned by the question. The boy listens to everything.

"I don't know," I say, "Let's try to work it out. Let's start at the beginning. How do you make that string?"

"I don't know," the boy says.

"Well," I say, "Then let's start at the beginning. The way we build our strings, any of them, is by *investing* in them. We don't just have an emotion, because emotion alone makes a very weak string. Instead, we build and create and then we use what we've created to make the spiritual string. Do you understand?"

He looks at me and then says, "Like when dad made the top of our tent by tanning animals' skins?"

"Exactly!" I say, "He worked and worked and then used what he worked on for the benefit of his family. He made the string between himself and all you children stronger."

The boy smiles widely.

"Do you know who did this first?"

"No," says the boy.

"Hashem," I say, "When he created for six days and then rested on the seventh. He invested in our world and then rested in it. And he created holiness as a result..."

"But He killed Nadav and Avihu."

"He did," I say, "So let's keep exploring. How do we, as people, create?"

"With our hands," the little boy answers.

"That's right," I say. I don't know what to say next. It seems I have reached a dead end. And then an idea strikes me.

"Do you remember when Moshe told us about which animals we can eat? Can you remember any of the rules for animals?"

My grandson thinks for a moment and then says, "Animals have to have split hooves and chew their cud."

"Very good!" I say, with a smile. "Now, do you know why?"

"No," he answers, a bit disappointed.

"That's okay," I say, "Let's think about our hands. If an animal has no fingers, can it create like us?"

"No," he says, "It can't."

"Right," I say, "And if it has lots of fingers, like we do?"

"Then it can create," he answers. "Like us."

"Right again," I say, with a smile. "Well, if it has lots of fingers, we shouldn't eat it. We'd be destroying an animal that can create like us and that would be a waste. We don't connect to G-d by destroying. He is the Creator, and we want to imitate Him. An animal with *no* fingers is too far from creation. But animals with split hooves? They have just the essence of creation. They have the symbolism of creation – but aren't *actually* creative. So, we can eat them and make them a part of us."

"Is this what the *KOHANIM* (priests) split their fingers, like cows, when they bless us?"

I think for a moment before answering. "Yes, I think so. *KOHANIM* aren't supposed to be creative like regular people. They are hampered, just like the cows. The *KOHEN'S* (priest's) job is to actually weave the string using the investments of the people."

After a pause, the boy asks, "So why do the animals need to choose their cud?" the boy asks.

"Ah," I say, the pieces clicking together, "Because when they chew their cud, they rest like we should on the Sabbath – living on what we've already acquired and resting with G-d. You can't just build and build, you have to dedicate what you make *to* something. This trait gives them the ability to contribute to the string of holiness."

The boy thinks for a while and then his eyes open wide. "Nadav and Avihu didn't do this right." he says.

"What do you mean?" I ask. I hadn't realized there was a connection.

"They only brought incense," the boy says, "My father taught me that incense represents emotion because smells make us feel things. But they didn't bring flour, which takes a lot of work to make. And they didn't bring oil, which takes a lot of purification to make. They didn't make the string the right way."

"You're right!" I say, surprised. I act delighted, but the image of those burning brothers is still seared into my mind.

"Can the birds help us understand more?" the boy asks.

I think for a moment, and then I realize the answer to his question.

"Well," I say, "We live in a world where our strings can connect to all sorts of things, even things that aren't real."

"What do you mean?" he asks.

"We could connect our strings to gods that don't exist," I say, "But when we do so, we think we're connecting to something real because so many strings go there. But only the connections would be real, not the thing they're connecting to. Those strings can't lift us up. We can even connect to ourselves. Actually, we do that a lot. When we do that, we often don't know we aren't *really* connecting to Hashem."

"What does this have to do with the birds?" he asks.

"Ah!" I say, "Remember when Moshe told us what birds we can and can't eat?"

"Yes..." says the boy, his voice trailing off.

"Did he give us a rule?"

"A rule?"

"Did he say something like, 'you can eat all the red ones?'"

"No," says the boy, "He just told us which birds we can eat and which ones we can't."

"Right," I say, "That's because birds are so close to Hashem's world. Hashem lives in a world without death and there's nothing dead in the sky. In order to draw close to Hashem, we aren't allowed to figure out what is holy or not. It is too tempting to pick whatever *we* already believe in. If we did that, the strings would actually connect right back to us. So, when we draw close to Hashem, *He* decides what's holy. The closer you get to G-d, the more He decides what's right."

I see the boy's thinking, and then he says, quietly, "Nadav and Avihu designed their own offering."

"You're right," I say, surprised again. "And we're so close to G-d, that we're not allowed to do that."

I am beginning to suspect that this is why Moshe had gone into all those strange laws. He might have been telling us what Nadav and Avihu had done wrong.

"What about the bugs?" the boy asks.

The bugs? I wonder. Could Moshe have intended a message even with the bugs? He always seemed to like symbolic riddles. I don't know where to start, so I ask the boy.

"Did you notice anything strange about the bugs?" I can't think of anything.

"Sure," says the boy, "He said they go on four legs. But bugs have *six* legs."

Trust a little boy to know that.

"Four legs...." I trail off, thinking. And then an idea comes to me, "My beautiful boy, what else does *arba*, or four, mean?"

"It means 'multiply'," says the boy.

"Right again," I say. "Maybe Moshe was saying that bugs go by multiplying. They don't act as individuals. They aren't driven to connect, by themselves. Instead, they act by teeming and producing generations of bugs. We can't bring that essence into ourselves. Some people do that, just multiplying like bugs but not acting with the individual will we need."

The boy looks thoughtful. "But what about the ones with jointed legs that jump? How come we can eat them?"

"Ah," I say, "When you want to go somewhere, how do you get there?"

"I run," says the boy.

"Yes, you run," I say, "With your legs. You can go places you choose to go because of your legs. You don't go places by multiplying, you do it by choosing and then using your legs to get there. Well, the bugs we can eat have legs like ours and they jump up, using those legs to go places and jump towards the heavens. In a way, those legs symbolize what our will should be, so they are closer to what we need to be. They have an essence that can be a part of a holy people. They are kind of like the split hooves, except for will instead of creative ability."

The boy whispers, "Nadav and Avihu were drunk."

"Yes, I know," I whisper back, filled with sadness. I'm not sure why he brought it up.

"I know how they got when they were drunk. It was like they weren't themselves. The wine took over."

"I know," I say.

"They were like the bugs with no legs," he says, "They didn't have their own will."

I just stare at him for a minute, stunned.

Were all of Moshe's laws teaching us to avoid the mistakes of Nadav and Avihu?

"Let's try the fish," I say, suddenly curious.

"Okay," says the boy.

"What's special about water?" I ask.

"Everybody always says it is spiritual," says the boy, "Which is why *SHAMAYIM* or 'heaven' literally means place of waters. And why Miriam's holiness gave us the well that travels with us."

"Very good!" I say, getting the beginning of an idea. "We are surrounded by spirituality, like a fish is surrounded by water."

"Okay," says the boy, closing his eyes and trying to imagine what that is like.

"We could be almost part of the water, with every part of us dedicated to moving through the water and connecting to it. But that isn't our job. We're supposed to be part of the spiritual world, but also separate from it. We travel through the spiritual world, but as physical beings. We aren't the strings; we are what the strings connect to."

"Okay…" says the boy.

"Well," I say, "The fins separate the core of the fish from the waters while the scales steer it through the waters. Its whole body isn't dedicated to steering through the spiritual world."

"Did Nadav and Avihu get this wrong?" he asks.

This time, *I* do have the answer. "They were priests; they were Kohanim. They are supposed to be our fins and our scales in the spiritual world, but not our body. Scales separate us. But they brought incense. They brought emotion. It is what normal people bring. They merged the scales with the body of the people. Even more than that, they brought *only* incense. They neglected the physical which is represented by the grain and the oil. Everything was dedicated to swimming through the waters – so they lacked fins as well. They became strings."

"So, they did that wrong too," the boy concludes.

"They did," I agree.

The boy still looks a little sad, and scared. I try to reassure him.

"G-d won't kill you," I say, "G-d won't kill you because you always act with will, like the bugs we can eat. And you recognize you are only supposed to be an interface to the spiritual world, like the fins and scales. And you let G-d define what is Holy as you draw close to Him, like the birds we can eat. And you embrace the cycle of holiness, like the animals we can eat."

I pause for a moment, letting it all sink in. Moshe had been giving a message to all of us. He had been giving us a physical mnemonic so we could avoid the fate of Nadav and Avihu. And he'd done it without ever criticizing the brothers themselves. He may not be good with people, but I can still appreciate what he's done.

"But how did killing Nadav and Avihu sanctify G-d?" the boy asks.

I draw in a long breath, "Their death showed us how to strengthen the string the right way. It helped all of us make a proper connection with G-d. And they became strings – wholly dedicated to that connection. It isn't our ideal, but it is a sanctification."

The boy just sits there, tears suddenly appearing in his eyes. I give him a long hug and whisper into his ear, "So long as you remember to connect only to Him, and so long as you do it the way He wants, G-d will grant you peace."

He's crying more now. I hold him. He's exhausted and I can feel the grief pouring out of his body.

After a long while, I feel him getting tired. I lay him down and he looks up with far more peaceful eyes. "Thank you, grandma Elisheva," he says, with a soft smile.

"Sleep well," I say, gently. "Sleep well, my little Pinchas (Phineas)."

And with that, his eyes close and he immediately begins to drift off.

Once he is asleep, I stand up and walk slowly from the tent.

He can sleep, but I cannot.

I am Elisheva, the wife of Aaron. And I have lost two of my sons this day.

I have watched the burnt bodies of my Nadav and Avihu being carried away. Even the quiet, beautiful, power of Pinchas' young face cannot wipe away my horror.

As I exit the tent, the cold night air strikes my face. And then I realize that while I might be able to *explain* why it happened, I will never be able to *understand* it.

Perhaps Pinchas will do better.

Pinchas grew up to be a prominent zealot for G-d. It is not hard to image that the death of his uncles served as a key formative memory.

Tazria-Metzora: The Assessors

The men in the white coats looked down on us from their windows. They had clipboards and were continually taking notes. What about, I had no idea, although we must have been the focus of those notes. The 'us' was a group of about 75 people, milling around aimlessly in a massive warehouse of a room. We all had bald heads and were wearing rough gray garments like a group of medieval monks. I had no idea what we were doing here. I mean, I know *why* I was there, but I had no idea *what* I was accomplishing by being there.

I didn't know what the men in the white coats wanted from us.

I'd been here for three weeks. I'd been incarcerated by make-believe lab technicians. Three weeks earlier, I'd been a god, CEO of a successful and growing company. I ate in the best restaurants, surrounded by the best people. But three weeks later? Three weeks later, I was trudging around in a rough smock, pointlessly circling an empty room, and eating the plain bread and water that the lab coats seemed to think was food.

Others had come and gone in the time I'd been here. Others had figured out what those men wanted, or at least what would convince them to release us. But I couldn't. I couldn't work out the logic of my situation.

It had all started a little over two months ago. I'd been at an industry conference. I work in digital security. But I wasn't just one of the participants, and it wasn't an ordinary conference. I was *the* keynote speaker, and it was an industry CEOs' conference. I wasn't just any kind of keynote speaker, I was the kind of keynote speaker who dashes into a conference at the last minute, puts on a song and dance and escapes out a back door before any of the regular CEOs can waste his precious time. It was quite an awarding experience. It was also entirely appropriate. My company was going places, it was taking risks, it was establishing new ground. The attendees were really nothings in comparison. None of them had any real spark to them. They were just your standard issue lemmings; showing up at all my presentations just so they could be near real greatness; as if listening to a lecture could somehow impact the drive they fundamentally lacked. Whether it was a lack of talent or a lack of hunger, they didn't have what it took to take on the world. I knew it. Deep down, so did they.

The first signs of trouble weren't long in coming. A man like me makes his living off information. Be it up-to-the-minute revenue reports or streams of industry content, I live off data and my ability to digest it, filter it and act on it at super-human speeds. I get a lot of information. Well, I had *gotten* a lot of information. I actually had a team that provided it to me. Fifteen analysts, collecting whatever they thought was relevant (each in their own domain) and then three gatekeepers ensuring there was no duplication in the news feed that sustained me. It wasn't cheap, but it was worth it. The relevant bit ticked past my screen in a millisecond "You have received a TSRAT score warning."

I had no idea what a TSRAT score was and so I simply disregarded the message. I just kept going with my day. I *was* a busy man.

But the TSRAT score didn't just go away.

The next message came a few days later. My driver had been racing me home, as he always does. I hate to waste time in the car. I hadn't really noticed what was going on, but I guess there were a few horns. Anyway, I got home and then I was texted again "You have received a second TSRAT warning."

I remember what I thought then. "Why the hell do I care?"

I was on the verge of firing the particular analyst who'd allowed the message through when I decided to ask him: "Why the hell do I care?" It wasn't very hard to do. I have a single button on my phone that sends that phrase instantly. It is generally a prelude to getting a new lemming. Sometimes (well... often), my people can be such incredible idiots. There's a reason they're followers and I'm the leader.

The analyst didn't do the smart thing. He didn't simply stop sending me stupid TSRAT notices. Instead, he actually replied, "I've heard bad things happen to people who don't care."

He forgot. I'm not 'people.'

I decided to ignore him.

But he didn't learn his lesson and shut up about the TSRAT. The next day, he sent another message "Your Total Social Rating AssessmenT (TSRAT) score has risen again. The Assessors say they're going to go public if you don't respond."

I hit the "Why the hell do I care" button. This time, the analyst wasn't stupid enough to actually reply. Maybe one of the other lemmings actually warned him what would come next.

I almost wish he had responded though. I mentioned that I get live cash flow updates, right? Well, I got one right then: a sudden dip in revenues. It was totally out of the blue. A 5% drop from normal averages adjusted for time of day, season and all the rest. At first, I just dismissed it as bad modeling. Not every predictive forecast can be perfect. But, an hour later, the deviation was 10%. Something was seriously wrong. Not only that, but the stock price of the company took an immediate 25% dive. 25% of the equity I'd created, had been wiped out in 60 minutes.

Suddenly, *all* the analysts were talking about the TSRAT. The TSRAT this, the TSRAT that. I flicked on the TV for an outsider's perspective. And there it was on CNBC: "TSRAT issues notice about LOCK-ME Inc. CEO James Buffalo."

I had no idea what the hell was going on.

They explained it. The TSRAT was some kind of social score. I didn't really know what the point was. As I saw it – you get the sheep in the world to want your product and you make money. It's that simple. Social value scoring systems are a joke to make the stupid feel happy about themselves. For some reason, it wasn't working quite the way I expected. Everybody – well, a lot of people – seemed to care about this TSRAT score.

It was when I looked up a list of previous targets that I knew what the 'Assessors' were up to. These people had a product. Some sort of idiotic social pressure. The customer wasn't the public. The customer was me. They were going to "assess" me until they bled me dry. I'd pay them whatever they wanted, and they'd back off. It was the classic business model: you get the sheep in the world to want your product and you make money. They were just more brutal than even I had been.

I wasn't a sheep. They'd learn that rather quickly.

Five minutes later, using my home studio, I was on CNBC. A minute after that, I was railing against whoever in the hell was behind this TSRAT thing. They were a bunch of scamming bastards, ginning up business by blackmailing successful people like me. I wasn't going to stand for it. I had a product people needed. Anybody who didn't care for blackmail, the customers and investors *I wanted*, would keep buying. My company was bigger than these two-bit hacks. I wasn't desperate, I wasn't begging. I was powerful and I was serving my customers.

It didn't work.

Somehow, these TSRAT people were taking me apart. By the end of the interview, revenues had plummeted even further. So had the stock price. This was a problem. I'm a leveraged guy. A highly leveraged guy. It is part of pushing the boundaries of what's possible. The problem with leverage is that bumps in the road can destroy you. If you can't meet your covenants, or you can't make your payments, you're done.

I stayed up all that night. I wasn't watching successes unfold. I was watching my world fall apart. Around 11, the lemming sent me a message: "The Assessors say they can fix everything. You just have to meet them."

I didn't want to meet them. Instead, I decided to figure out who they were. But all I could find was that they were selected on the basis of some sort of analysis of their social scores. I dug and I dug. I had my people ask every question they could think of. But I worked out exactly nothing. They seemed to be a black box. I had no idea why so many people followed their boycotts.

I hoped I could outlast it, but I only had 5 days before a significant debt payment was due. And I knew, almost immediately, that I wasn't going to have the cash. The only good thing was that my lemmings were quitting in droves, cutting my outflows substantially.

It took three days for me to give in. I asked for an address, and they gave me one. It led to a massive and hulking warehouse. I entered a dimly lit conference room. Then I waited. I waited for three hours until, finally, a man in a white coat entered the room.

I asked them how much they wanted. They ignored me. I guessed they were just playing for higher stakes. I was surprised when they told me they'd make it all stop. All I had to do was stay there, in the warehouse, until they decided I could leave.

I asked if I'd be able to make the monthly debt payment. And they assured me I could. If all else failed, they'd make it themselves. It was an odd form of blackmail.

I agreed to their terms.

It was then that they took my clothes, my phone and my computer. They shaved my head and then they gave me a rough gray robe. Then they left me there, amongst a crowd of other victims. There were no locks on the doors. We were free to leave whenever we wanted. But the implications of *that* decision were clear.

Others had been there for months. Their eyes were angry and resentful. I talked to them. They were lemmings, all of them. None of them knew what was happening or why. Others barely had time to warm up their robes before they left. I never knew who would be released in advance, but nobody seemed to shout "I've got it" moments before their escape.

The entire time, of course, I worried about what I've built. I worried about my business. They interviewed me every day, sometimes several times a day. I couldn't figure out what they wanted, though. I couldn't seem to negotiate my way out of their trap. I was sure, after a week, that everything I'd built was gone. Nobody else could run my enterprise.

It was during the third week that they let me see something of the outside world. There was a newscast, CNBC again. The idiot lemming who told about TSRAT was being interviewed. He was identified as the "Provisional CEO."

I watched him for a minute before I realized what the Assessors were showing me. The business was alive. It wasn't quite flourishing. It wasn't doing quite as well as it had before. But it was far from dead. The lemming was doing a decent job.

They didn't ask me any questions that day, they just let me go back to the big room. I left, utterly confused about what was going on. I still didn't know what they wanted.

I went back to the big room, with the others. I circled just like them. I thought. Then I had my "aha" moment.

I suddenly realized what it is all about. Less than a minute later, they pulled me off the floor.

As I sat in the conference room, the men in the white jackets watched me, waiting for me to speak. And I did. I told them what I'd learned. I told them I'd realized the lemmings aren't just lemmings and I'm not a god. I told them I realized those around me made everything work. I told them that I recognized, in a flash of insight, that I had defined myself – the core of myself – as a superior being. Now I realized it might not be true. Others might not have had my gifts or drive, but they all could contribute *something*.

I told them that I knew now that the rest of humanity was not simply made up of lemmings and sheep.

They gave me back my phone. They gave me back my computer. They gave me back my clothes. And then they gave me a small medallion. It had a sequoia, flowing waters, a flying bird and rays of light.

I asked them what it meant, and they told me. It represented my rebirth. The sequoia represented deep roots, the waters represented change and renewal, the flying bird represented the ability to rise above the weakness of the world and the rays of light represented the presence of a higher power.

"Because" they explained, "there is always a higher power."

I walked out of the warehouse, both humbled and raised up.

My business bounced back. The stain of the TSRAT went as quickly as it came. Unlike any other social media boycott, when it was lifted, it was gone without a trace. It was almost like the world around me was rewarding those who found their way through the Assessors' world.

In the end, I did give the Assessors money. It wasn't a blackmail payment though. It was a contribution. I contributed so that they could help others rise above their hubris.

The Torah Readings of *TAZRIA-METZORA* deal with the mysterious ailment of *TZARAT*. It has a few suggestive causes. It strikes stone houses – those with permanence. It seems to be hidden at first, but then revealed. It requires those who are struck to seek out the *KOHANIM* (priests) for relief. When it strikes clothes, their fabrics are insulted and lowered. And those who are struck's are exiled from the camp and required to say "unclean, unclean" again and again.

There are many discussions about what *TZARAT* is. I think it was a mold – it could strike buildings, clothes and people. But it had a purpose. Its purpose was to strike down hubris. Why else would the sufferers need to repeat "unclean" if they are surrounded by other "unclean" people in a place designated for them? Who are they speaking to, other than G-d and themselves? Fundamentally, for me, *TZARAT* would strike those who imagined themselves to be fundamentally greater than those around them. Their belief could come out as *LASHON HARA* (gossip), or it could take many other forms. *TZARAT* takes those who suffer from it down a notch. It is in keeping with many other parts of the Torah – parts that emphasize the evils which attend "men of name."

The TSRAT score in the story does the same thing. The judges are chosen from those who do not exhibit this sort of hubris. The process is the same as that in the Torah. Those who suffer must seek out experts. They must submit to them. They must accept what they cannot, themselves, diagnose. And they are freed when they recognize their limits.

At the end of the Biblical *TZARAT* process, a living bird is dipped in the blood of a bird which has been killed over waters of life. It is mixed with cedar, *TOLA'AT SHANI* and *AYZOV*. The cedar represents deep roots, the *TOLA'AT SHANI* represents G-d's faith to us and the

AYZOV represents the ability to flow and change. The water of life represents our ability to be spiritually renewed – water takes away toxins and brings nutrients. Fundamentally, the living bird represents our potential. We can soar towards the skies – a place without death and destruction. But we can only soar if we realize our limits. By dipping the live bird in the dead one, the *TZARAT* sufferer is shown that he can soar precisely because he has come to understand the limits of his mortal self.

The symbolism of the cleansing processing goes beyond this. The touching of the bird's blood to the ear (influences), thumb (actions) and toe (will) reinforce the idea that this newfound humility is made a part of the sufferer's reality. Finally, the shaving of the head diminishes the sufferer's individuality – stunting their personal pride.

In the end the sufferer of *TZARAT* is lifted up. Not in a relative sense – but in absolute terms. They are better than they were, even as they recognize the infinite distance between themselves and Hashem.

Acharei-Kedoshim: Fat Ladies

It was already dark outside when Sarah Hastings looked around the library's classroom. The room itself was grand, especially for such a small town. However, like so many other things she'd encountered on her trip through the unwanted parts of America, it had a sense of tremendous wear hanging over it. Sarah's host had explained the history, unbidden. The library had been built with timber money during a long-ago boom. The building had been beautiful, but the town had no way to maintain it. Which is why it had gone through a long and relentless process of decline.

Sarah expected this description would apply to the people as as well as it applied to the library they had built.

It always did.

Sarah took her seat at the front of the room. There was a little microphone there. Arrayed in front of her were close to a hundred chairs: the old wooden folding kind. They were lined up carefully, precisely, by a librarian still desperate to show the pride of this fading town.

The room was empty, except for Sarah and her host – a huge woman named Margaret. Sarah never liked to show up late for these things. She figured it was disrespectful to her audience. They'd had enough disrespect already.

Gradually, as Sarah watched, the women began to trickle into the room. They didn't approach her. They eyed her from a distance, still uncertain whether they had the courage to talk to *the* Sarah Hastings. Sarah didn't push herself on them. In time, she knew, they would come to her.

They always did.

Within twenty minutes, the room was full. In the back, a few more people stuffed into every space that was available to them. The room was bloated with people. It was rated for 112 people, according to the fire marshal. He couldn't have meant *these* 112 people. Because, while Sarah was pleasantly plump, every other woman in the room was downright huge.

As Sarah looked around, they chatted quietly, uncomfortably. It was their nature, Sarah knew. She saw the furtive, and excited, glances in her direction. She smiled at one and all. And then she looked at her watch, and – at exactly 8:00PM – she stood up from her seat, picked up her microphone, and said exactly one sentence.

"I was 150 pounds on my twelfth birthday."

She let the words hang there for a moment. They flew around the room and, in an instant, there was total silence. It didn't used to work that way, but now it did.

"150 pounds," she repeated, "For those who don't know, that's like the 115th percentile."

There were a few scattered laughs. Not everybody got the joke, and not everybody realized she was joking.

"My parents talked like it was just a phase. I hoped they were right. But we all knew they weren't right. It wasn't a phase. My parents, Jon and Rachel, were massive people. The neighborhood kids even invented a new word to describe them 'Obeast.' 'Obese' wasn't enough for them. They were a special target of mockery and insult. They were also my future, and I knew it."

Sarah saw the knowing nods around the room. She took a small sip of water and then continued, "At 13, my body began to change – in earnest. But while other 13-year-old girls hoped boys would notice – I hoped they wouldn't. Some girls went for revealing clothes, trying to push the bounds of what their schools and their parents would allow. I went in the opposite direction. I just covered more and more of myself until all you could see was a bundle of fabric where a young lady should have been.

"But I wasn't a young lady. I was some kind of freak. There were others like me. We began to glom together. Not like real friends, but like diseased lepers with nobody else to talk to. We weren't *real* friends; we were *fat* friends. We didn't talk about anything but our weight. We couldn't get past it. As we got more and more embarrassed by our bodies, we began to drift away; even from each other. You ladies already know this story, right?"

Heads nod in agreement.

"Y'all have lived it, right?"

More heads nod, more emphatically this time.

"I know you do," answered Sarah, "But I need you to know *I* know it too. I started dieting then, at 13. Not the light 'I think I'll skip the cookies' type of diet, but hard-core dieting. I lost weight, each time. And then, inevitably, I put it all back on. All of it, and some more, each and every time. I was getting bigger and bigger and bigger. At my sweet 16, I was 195 lbs. I wasn't a tall girl either; I was 5'4". Those same boys who mocked my parents mocked me too. I didn't merit a clever word though. I was just 'SWAT.' It was short for She Weighs A Ton.

"I guess if the weight alone had been my problem that would have been okay. But weight weighs so much more than you can measure on a scale. It didn't carry just the mockery or exclusion either. It carried hopelessness. It bled into every part of my life. I felt like if I couldn't conquer *this*, I couldn't conquer *anything*. With every diet I failed at, my ability to push back was dented just a little bit more. It was like the *Fat* was killing whatever *Fight* I had in me. Forget success. Forget a husband or kids. I was 16 and I was done for. Worst of all, I knew it."

Sarah caught the sight of not a few mournful faces. They *knew* what she'd gone through. They were *still* going through it.

"I finished high school, but I couldn't face college. I got a dead-end job at a big box store. The aisles were wide. It must seem crazy to a regular person, but that actually mattered to me. I got myself some of those huge, padded, shoes. My favorite jobs were all in the back though. I didn't want people to see me as I struggled to stock shelves. Even worse was talking to customers. Almost everyone would look at me with that horrible combination of pity and judgment. Like 'what an awful struggle that girl must be going through' was combined with 'I never would have let it get that far.' The worst part wasn't the criticism. The worst part was that I believed they were right. *They* hadn't let it get that far, so I believed something was wrong with *me*, and with *my willpower*.

"My only comfort, if you want to call it that, was that I knew it wouldn't last long. I wasn't yet 20, but I knew I'd end up getting one of those motorized wheelchairs before I reached 35. And, on my bad days, I looked forward to it. I wanted to be shut in. I wanted to waste away where nobody could see me."

Sarah pauses, takes a deep breath and then whispers, "On my bad days, I wanted to die."

Sarah stops, takes another drink. Looks around the room at knowing faces. She still remembers that pain.

"And then, one day," Sarah continues in a soft voice, "a woman came into my store."

Unbidden, tears spring into Sarah's eyes.

"She was a woman who seemed to see my soul. She saw right through me. There was no 'what an awful struggle.' There was no 'I never would've let it go that far.' There was just a look that said, 'I can help.' I saw that woman, and she saw me, and I just cried. Right there in the middle of the big box store. I just cried. And then that woman invited me to Bible Study. I wasn't a religious person, not in any way. But if she'd invited me to go climb Mount Everest, I would've signed right up. She was like a lifeboat to me, just then. She was, I kid you not, saving my life.

"I showed up at Bible Study. And the very first lesson was about Leviticus. That woman was teaching the class. And she read, 'You shall not uncover the nakedness of your near kin.' And I thought, 'well, duh.'"

There were a few laughs.

"But the woman continued. 'The Bible,' she said, "Doesn't use euphemisms. Not long before this verse it gives commands concerning a man who lies with a woman with semen. This isn't meant to be gentle stuff. So why does it say *uncover the nakedness*?'"

Sarah looked around the room, but there weren't any answers there, just anticipation.

"Well," said Sarah, "That teacher, that woman who saved my life, explained it. She said the Hebrew word was ERVAT. It was used by Joseph to accuse his brothers of being spies. He said they were seeking out the ERVAT of Egypt. They were seeking out its *weakness*. Nakedness, that woman explained, was weakness."

Sarah paused. And then added, "I think y'all know that feeling."

She saw tears in the eyes of a few of the masses of women who were there.

"I went home that night, to investigate. Why didn't the Bible want us to uncover the nakedness of our close relatives? Other than the whole 'gross' bit. I thought, maybe there's a story here, to explain it all. I looked back until I found something before the laws. It was something *I* could relate to. It was a story. The story of the death of the sons of Aaron. And after that story there were all sorts of laws. Laws about the food you eat. Laws about keeping yourself pure. Laws about the exclusion of leprosy. Laws about atonement. And laws about nakedness. And I thought, we've got food, social exclusion and nakedness as weakness. These laws, I realized, were all about *me*."

"I poked and I prodded. And the more I poked and prodded, the more I felt impurity and sin were somehow tied up with one another. Then I found the first sin. Not the apple in the garden, the Bible never calls *that* a sin. I found sin, CHAIT, waiting outside Cain's door, waiting to pounce. And I thought, I *know* sin. *Sin* is what made me the way I am. *Sin* is the temptation to destroy – yourself or others. It is temptation so strong you can't overcome it. But G-d promises Cain he *can* overcome it. He promises Cain that when he does, he will be a better person."

"I couldn't understand that. *How* could Cain defeat sin?"

"I went to more Bible study groups. I listened. I watched that incredible woman. And she watched me. Slowly, I began to feel more like a human. I still had no control over my weight, though. I was still the largest woman in the room, by a literal *wide* margin. But then, I read in Leviticus chapter 16: '…he shall take of the congregation of the children of Israel two he-goats for a sin-offering…' and I thought: there's sin there. There's temptation there. But what sin and what temptation? Nadav and Avihu were punished. Nothing else had happened. What sin remained?"

"And then I realized it was the sin of *rebellion*. The people wanted to rebel against what they'd seen. They couldn't understand it. They were stained. Temptation was waiting at their door. But it hadn't entered. It hadn't yet made them *carry* the weight of what the Torah calls AVON."

"And then, one day, everything clicked together."

"The laws about food were about reaching towards G-d and walking in His ways. The laws about leprosy were about making yourself physically aware of when you were so full of self-regard that you left no space for what was truly important."

"The law of the scapegoat was about knowing there were two paths. One led to nothingness in the wilderness while the other led to communion with a timeless G-d. This law is called a *KAPER*, an atonement. It is first used when Noah is putting pitch on the Ark so the water can't get through. Atonement is pitch for the soul. It protects against *AVON*, the weighty after-effects of sin."

"The next laws, the laws about not slaughtering potential sacrifices in a field were about not wasting potential. Even an *animal* doesn't deserve to just die when it can serve a higher purpose."

"And the laws about covering nakedness were about protecting yourself from your own weakness. And then, at the very end, are a few extra laws. There's one about not worshipping a god called Moloch who shares every letter in his name with the King, but who isn't the King. And it is followed by laws about sexual relationships that aren't quite right. These laws are about not twisting what is actually right."

"I saw this pattern and I realized that it spoke to *me*."

Sarah saw a few confused faces. She raised her free hand, defensively, "Don't worry, I'll explain. You see, I saw a path to my own redemption. Through food, I could keep myself focused on my mission. The laws about leprosy were about marking when I thought *just about me*, without realizing how much more than *me* I could be. After all, focusing on yourself is the truest path to exclusion."

"The law of the scapegoat showed me that I had to see, in my own mind's eye, the two paths before me. I had to, on a regular basis, take the time to see the big picture. The laws about not wasting potential sacrifices showed me that I could not let any potential be squandered. The laws about covering nakedness showed that I could not think about or explore my own weakness – I had to hide it away by focusing on other things. And the laws about twisting truth were about not cheating when it comes to what is right."

"This became my diet. Eat foods that fulfilled my mission – to be a strong and confident young woman. Keep a physical reminder of when I forgot about my greater potential because I was too busy serving my own wants. Keep the big picture in mind, knowing where the paths of my life lead. Know that I cannot waste myself or others. Avoid exploring my own weaknesses, by not tempting myself or dwelling on what I cannot accomplish. And forever forbid myself from twisting the rules in order to sidestep what I know is right."

"That's became my process. I didn't lose weight suddenly. I didn't track my progress on a scale. Instead, I kept to that path for three long years. Slowly and surely, I improved. Until, one day, I realized I had gotten where I needed to be. I was a confident young woman. And while I knew that my battle with sin, with temptation, would never end, I also knew that each time I won that battle, I became greater because of it. I knew that I was no longer marked like Cain – to live like an animal in the field. Instead, I could live with others and be part of my community. And I could be *stronger* than those who had never faced such temptation. I had faced the test of Cain, and *I* had overcome it. And, most importantly, I no longer thought of the sweet release of death."

"I realized all of that on one day in August, four years ago. I realized that day, that this process was more than a way of losing weight; it was a way of changing my life. And then I realized what I had to do. I realized I had to share what I'd learned – not just keep it for myself. I realized I had to travel and speak to women like you. I realized that my true potential wasn't in being a strong and confident young woman. No, my true potential was all about unlocking the power in *you*. It was about unleashing the potential that has been growing in all of you, year after year – with every battle you *lost* against the destructive temptation we call 'sin'."

Sarah looked around, smiling and sharing the confidence she felt with the others in the room.

"And so," Sarah continued, "I began to travel. From town to town, all across America, I've been travelling ever since. Every night, I've spoken in some new town, in some new place. The fact is: this sort of truth doesn't travel by Facebook or YouTube. This sort of truth travels, from woman to woman, in person. I could share a video online if all I wanted was to share the process. But I want to do more. I don't want you to *just* be strong and confident women. I want you to be *like me*. I want you to unlock the strength of other women who are losing their war against temptation."

Sarah paused and then almost whispered, "I want you all to discover your true potential. And I want what I've learned to spread like a positive virus, renewing and rejuvenating everybody it touches."

Sarah smiled, grinning from ear to ear, and then put her microphone down.

The room exploded in applause.

As she looked at the energized mass of morbidly obese women, one thought crossed her mind: "These fat ladies are gonna rule the world."

Emor: The Priesthood

Before I enter the parking lot, I check it furtively, glancing around in order to ensure I won't be seen. In the dimly lit building next to the lot, there is activity. But the lot itself, cast in darkness and devoid of cars, seems completely safe.

I realize this is my chance. I rush towards the front door of the building and then carefully set my bundle on the ground outside of it. Then, just as quickly, I turn and vanish into the night.

It is the hardest thing I've ever done.

I am the Chairwoman of the Buckel Foundation and arguably the most powerful person in the entire world.

My very power is what has driven me to do this terrible thing.

On April 14th, 2018, my life was transformed. I was a socially aware 17-year-old. Even at that stage of my life, I knew I had so much caring to give others – my mother-spirit was bursting with it. But I also knew it wasn't enough simply to share my spirit in all directions. I knew I needed something *specific* to care for. A million causes tugged at me, but I could not possibly serve them all. I was too practical for that.

I needed *one*.

I needed one thing I could pour my life into, and thus find *true* fulfillment.

That morning, on my way to a protest to protect a neighborhood park, I saw a horrifying headline on my Twitter feed. It changed my life. It read, simply: "Prominent Gay Rights Lawyer Self-Immolates in Environmental Protest." The man's name had been David Buckel and he had given everything for a cause he deeply believed in. He had set himself aflame, with fossil fuels, to demonstrate the danger than fossil fuels pose to the planet itself.

Buckel's action inspired me. I went to the protest, but my mind was a million miles away. Suddenly, I knew what I would dedicate my mother-spirit to.

I would dedicate it to Mother Earth.

That is what I did. My education, my internships, my activism, my every waking hour, were dedicated to the environment.

Before long, I had self-identified with one of the strongest wings of the environmental movement.

We had a simple motto: "Leave no trace."

You may have heard of it as a guiding principle of a camping movement. But for us, it was more. We would leave no trace and so the world around us would be returned to a perfect state of nature. What we believed in wasn't a faith or a creed. It was necessity. It was truth. It was the salvation of the planet itself.

We knew something vital, something beautiful, was being destroyed by human hands.

We weren't fools, of course. We knew we were the cutting edge of humanity. We knew "leave no trace" was an aspiration even for us and so it would be a near impossibility for humanity as a whole. Nonetheless, we felt we could bend the curve in that direction and thus make the world a better place, if not a perfect one. So, we preached, and we spoke, and we talked. And we learned how to express ourselves in ways that earned us a steady trickle of devotees. We graduated to arguing and cajoling and sharing and demanding. With all that effort, *all* we secured was a steady trickle of devoted lovers of Earth. We did not succeed in fundamentally changing the course of mankind. We felt helpless as we watched the world unravel, despite the solutions we held within our tightknit group.

Then I had an idea. I realized people needed fulfillment and they needed pride. To satisfy this, I created a system of certification so people could be rated based on their actions in support of Mother Gaia and their understanding of the planet's needs.

The idea was simple, if you were truly dedicated to the Earth, you would make the most fundamental of sacrifices to Her: you would sacrifice your *time* for Her benefit. We would honor you for it.

The certification system was set up like a ladder. Aspiring Guardians of Gaia would start their climb up the ladder with new efforts to recycle and with the completion of basic educational modules. Accomplish these tasks and you could achieve a temporary rating by our movement. You would be known as a Guardian of Gaia 1st class. Your rank and its duration would reflect your commitment to the planet.

The ranks climbed from there. They piled on new sacrifices and educational opportunities. As they climbed, Guardians were pulled away from processed food, having more than one child, using plastic or relying on fossil fuel vehicles. But they could climb yet higher. By ending their use of all fossil fuels (even for electricity), by using only biodegradable building materials, by committing to having *no* children whatsoever, and by devoting their resources to the support of our world-embracing efforts, they could rise ever higher.

As they climbed these ladders, greater understanding was granted to the Guardians. They moved beyond the simple science of the environment and into the far deeper spiritual understanding of Mother Gaia herself. As they climbed, they could connect to the true life-source of our world.

Of course, the highest level remained beyond the strength of most. That level required the sacrifice of *all* of one's future time in service of Gaia. The highest level required one to follow in the footsteps of David Buckel himself. When a Guardian reached that pinnacle, many outside the movement saw a needless death. But we knew that those who gave themselves up were joined in spirit with Mother Gaia – living forever in the spiritual biosphere of our Earth Mother. The fact was that those who could not muster the courage for that final leap were jealous of those who had done so.

Guardians were more than just educated and recognized. They were also granted the power to lead others up the ladder. They themselves could be the gatekeepers of our great movement.

With this new system, our movement exploded. Tens and then hundreds of millions joined and began their slow ascent in the service of Mother Earth. With our numbers, and our dedication, came political power. Initially, our certification experts were called upon to bless projects large and small. Then we were asked to rate whole communities and businesses. Finally, we were given the ability both to propose laws and to enforce them. We grew stronger and stronger.

There were those who accused us of creating a false religion. They claimed we promoted meaningless acts to the naïve and gave people false pride by claiming they were saving the planet. There were those who claimed we only existed to suck away the marrow of modern man in service to a false vision of an unchanging and far more beautiful natural world.

We knew we dealt in symbols. We also knew even our symbolic sacrifices were steppingstones in building our dedication to the Mother Spirit. These symbols served a greater truth. These symbols could not be undermined. This was why, to protect the movement, we used our ever-increasing power to crush the few deniers in our path.

Our movement was a success. Gradually, the world improved just as we had hoped it would. Lights were turned off. Cars were switched off. Natural materials were returned to their proper place. Industrial farming was brought to its knees. The excess of 'plenty' disappeared and was replaced with the nourishing acceptance of 'enough.'

The world was better for it.

I had sat at the epicenter of it all. I had founded the movement and named it after David Buckel. I had built the rankings and the tests and the demands. And in the course of my voyage, I made every commitment the organization demanded.

I was the public face of fundamental change.

As the reach of the Guardians extended, we were granted authority by almost every government. Our devotees bent their own religions in support of our cause – they found texts to reinforce our most fundamental beliefs. We had built something even the greatest Popes of Rome could only dream of. Ours was a truly global movement, reaching across national and religious lines and knitting humankind together in dedication to something greater than any single species.

But there was a shadow hovering over everything I did. As each new pinnacle was realized, I expected my mother-spirit to finally be fulfilled by the love it was sharing with Mother Earth.

It never was, though.

Then, slowly, gradually, I realized what my mother-spirit truly wanted. It wanted me to be a *mother*.

It wanted, *desperately*, for me to leave a trace.

That was a demand I could not accept.

The demand tore at me. I meditated on it for countless hours. I questioned how I could possibly deny my own beliefs so completely. I tore at myself, trying to excise the desire from my heart. But it remained, steadfast and resolute.

Others, close to my rank, had been required to provide documentation of sterilization. But I had been the first to ascend. All I had needed to give was a vow. I could have a child, secretly, I chose an unsuspecting man – a member of the public with no certification at all – and I carried out the ultimate betrayal of my beliefs.

I became pregnant.

I spent my pregnancy in my small apartment. I communicated by phone. I hid myself away and slowly gave form to a new life within my growing body. I reveled in the joy of it. I grimaced through the challenges of it. I hated myself for my decision to pursue it.

I considered abortion, but I feared the risk of the sin of conception, my sin, being uncovered.

When the time came, I delivered the child. I did it myself, quaking in fear at the risk of it. I feared I would die, and my baby would die, and my deception would be discovered. I feared I would lose everything.

I knew that if I did, I would deserve it.

The fears were overwrought. The baby was delivered safely. A beautiful young girl. A young girl I found I loved. But her birth only created another quandary. A pregnancy could be hidden. A child was something quite a bit harder to conceal.

In those first hours, I agonized over the options I had.

I could try to conceal the child. But a concealed child would be a stunted child. My love was too great for that.

I could allow others to know my failing. But if I were discovered, my movement and my planet would suffer irreparable harm. And my child and I would be banished and censured as traitors against the most powerful organization on Earth. We would be exiled by humankind. That was no kind of option.

There was a third path: I could die with my child and join her in the highest pantheon of dedication to Gaia. But I was not ready to kill her.

Then I realized there was one more path. I could, under cover of darkness, try to rid myself of her – and hope that those who found her raised her up with love and with care.

This was the path I chose. It was the only path my mother-spirit could accept.

I left my home and followed darkened and empty streets – streets my movement had darkened and emptied. At long last, I arrived at the city's largest hospital. I swept through its empty parking lot and left my child before its dimly lit doors. Then, I disappeared.

Even as I stride away, I realize that I have abandoned my child, but my child has not abandoned me. With her short newborn cries, she calls to my mother-spirit, demanding that I turn back.

But I cannot turn back. I cannot betray what I believe.

When I get home, I am desperate for salvation.

I know what I must do. Opening my computer, I find and fill out the paperwork necessary to start the adoption process. We Guardians of Gaia cannot add human life to a world too full of it. But this does not prevent us from raising those who have been brought into this life through no fault of their own.

I can adopt.

And maybe, just maybe, the stars will align, and I will adopt the girl I have just abandoned.

Maybe, just maybe, I could be a mother to my own child.

The Torah reading of *EMOR* talks about the limits of *KOHANIM* (priests). As the representatives of a people who embrace creation and flee from loss and destruction, the *KOHANIM* are kept distant from the loss of physical and spiritual potential. In many ways, this forces hard – almost inhuman – choices on them. Their human desires are curtailed. As only two of the most prominent examples: they may love a woman but be unable to marry her because she is a widow or divorcee; and they may lose a relative but be unable to pay final respects because death is always kept at a distance.

To help us understand these hard choices, I decided to write about a distinctly modern (and yet ancient) form of priesthood – the priesthood of Mother Earth. I tried to share how such a priesthood would function, sacrificing time in service of nature and encouraging symbolic activity among the lay population. And I tried to imagine the choices, the hard and almost inhuman choices, such a priesthood would face given the underlying values they stood for.

The *KOHANIM* and the Guardians serve very different masters, but there are parallels in the sacrifices their movements demand.

p.s. David Buckel, a real-life, 60-year-old, civil rights lawyer and environmentalist, did self-immolate on Saturday April 14th, 2018. That part of the story is not fictional. He did it to draw attention to the dangers of fossil fuels.

Behar: Concerto in C Minor

I close my eyes and ready myself for the opening notes of Vivaldi's Cello Concerto in C Minor. I know them by heart; I know the entire piece by heart. I've heard it thousands of times.

Nonetheless, even before the bows of the cellists strike their strings, I know there is something unusual about this night. There is something different. This performance will stand out from all the others.

I smile to myself, suddenly aware of how distant I was from this world seventeen years earlier. I smile to myself, amazed at how overwhelmingly this world has become intertwined with my soul.

I had been nineteen years old and sleeping off a hangover when the call came. It was 8:45AM on November 3rd, 1999. The number one song on the radio, that whole year, had been Prince's "Party like its 1999." It had spoken about Judgment Fay.

That was just about how the year had felt to me.

In January, after a long battle with breast cancer, my mother had died. In June, my father was claimed by a heart attack that surprised no one. I'd been in college, nominally studying mathematics. But the two strikes had hit me hard and I'd taken a leave of absence. I wanted to tackle my issues. All I actually did was drink. I woke up every morning hung over and spent every night trying to pretend to be happy.

Just about the only thing that had brought me joy was my half-brother. Edgar was ten years older than me. My father had been married before and Edgar had been the product of what I'd heard was an incredibly flawed relationship. As long as I had known him, Edgar had been an extraordinary musician. When he touched his violin, he gave depth and meaning to a world that all too often seemed shallow and material. It was like he uncovered a truth that nobody else could see. That year, the world had seemed to empty around me, but Edgar's music was able to fill it up. His music, alone, embraced me.

Unless you land with some big city philharmonic, the life of a musician is rarely static. You can't stay in one place and expect the crowds to come to you. The life of a musician is travel. I'd only see Edgar, his wife and his child, once every few months. Edgar, every time, would play something for me. I loved it. We all did. Edgar's son, Jonathan, would close his eyes and sway to the music, letting it fill him up. Of course, every time, Edgar would eventually stop playing. Every time, he'd leave again; he and his family would drive away to another concert in another city. Every time, knowing it was going to happen, destroyed me. Those nights, I would leave his small apartment, I would leave his music, and I would get wrecked.

Edgar and his family had left that morning. I'd heard him play the night before and, true to my pattern, I had drunk myself into an incredible stupor. I don't even know how I got home. But I did. Then, at 8:45 in the morning, I got the call.

Edgar and his wife had died in a car crash; a tire had blown out on their old beater of a van. They'd careened into oncoming traffic.

Jonathan, their son, was the only survivor.

Jonathan had no other living relatives. There were no grandparents. There was just me: an uncle with a shattered life.

I'd managed to sober up almost instantly. The responsibility demanded it. Those early days had been tough, though. Jonathan had been badly injured. He was only two years old, but it was obvious that something terrible had happened to him. At first, we feared brain damage. Before long, though, we discovered something else, something almost as bad for a child of Edgar. As the doctors had put it, he had suffered a "transverse fracture of petrous bone" and that had led to "peripheral sensorineural hearing loss."

A child of Edgar, the great musician, was profoundly deaf. His deafness could not be repaired.

I wanted to drink then. I didn't know what else to do. But I stopped myself. Or rather, the responsibility stopped me. When the boy was released from the hospital, he moved in with me. My brother had a life insurance policy, but not a huge one. I gathered the proceeds, dedicated in trust to his son, and I tried to figure out what to do.

The kid was traumatized. The kid was deaf. The kid had suffered incredibly. All I could think of was him swaying to his father's music the night before his world had been shattered. All I could think of was that somehow *this* child, this profoundly deaf child, *needed* to be a musician.

I tried to hire a music teacher. Every teacher we met was polite and understanding. They were consistent, though. Every one explained that a deaf child could not be a musician. I asked them about Beethoven, and they said his became deaf late in life, and there were questions about how deaf he'd actually been. No, they were quite sure; a deaf child could not be a musician.

I decided to become his teacher. I didn't know much about classical music, but there was one piece that had spoken to me, even when Edgar hadn't been the one playing it. It was Vivaldi's Cello Concerto in C Minor. It was a cello piece. And so, I bought two cellos. One for me and one for him. Then, while he was at a special day care for deaf children, *I* went to the music teachers. Bit by bit, *I* learned to play.

I would then come home, day after day, and I would try (using my idiot's version of sign language) to teach my deaf nephew to play the cello.

He could *see* me playing. But he couldn't hear enough even to criticize my lack of talent. I got him to hold the bow and draw it across the strings. He couldn't tell what he was doing, though. He couldn't *hear* the cacophony he was causing.

Once again, I looked for teachers, but I failed to find any who were willing to take him on. They all advised me to find something more appropriate for the struggling boy.

I saw a future, though. I saw a future where he could play. I couldn't help but keep going. Jonathan was another story. He would get mad at me. He would scream with his malformed words. He would hit me. He didn't *want* to learn. He hated me. Eventually, I came to the verge of giving up.

That was when I came across an article online. It described something called the Thalescope. It would scan a room in the visual range and convert what it saw to sound. A blind person, using the Thalescope, could be given some limited version of sight. The idea was a revelation to me. Perhaps I could flip it on its head. Perhaps I could give visual reality to what Jonathan could not hear.

I began to work on the concept. I developed software that performed that basic task. I boiled down what it showed, generating standing waves that represented notes. I played for Jonathan and had him watch a screen. I saw the glimmerings of understanding.

He played then, just a discordant series of notes. But, as I watched, he then adjusted and learned and tuned himself to play single notes – pure notes on his little cello. The sound was a revelation to me. More importantly, the sight was a revelation to him.

I kept working and learning. My software improved. I superimposed the notes of sheet music. I used colors for octaves and managed to show transitions between notes on the screen. Jonathan was able to see the patterns of the waves and how they would intersect. He could see the pleasing ratios of harmonies and overtones. He could see the relationships of the notes changing over time. We were learning together. He was learning to see music and I was learning how to show it to him.

More importantly, bit by bit, he was learning to play.

We went back to the teachers another time. They insisted, once again, that he could not play. But then he did, and they *all* wanted to teach him. They all wanted the honor of having taught a deaf boy to play. But something about the idea disturbed me. I didn't want Jonathan to be a *deaf boy* who could play. I wanted Jonathan to be a *musician* who could do what his father had done: bring depth and meaning to a world that seemed to lack it.

We went home, abandoning the teachers. Jonathan kept playing. Before long, though, it was clear there was nothing else I could teach him. He grew frustrated again. We had hit a wall and there was nothing I could do.

We were riding the subway, signing to one another, him angrily expressing his frustrations with music, when a young woman walked up to us. She was bright, in every respect. I know it's clichéd, but she was like a splash of sunlight on the subway. She smiled at me and asked, gently, why a deaf child was so enthralled by music. I told her our story and she told me hers. Her name was Eve. Her brother had been deaf. She'd learned to sign. But she was, herself, a cellist. A concert cellist. She explained that she'd never had a student, but she wanted Jonathan to be her first.

I remember asking her why. I wondered to myself, was she simply another ego-seeker seeking a trophy student? She gave me the perfect answer, though. She said she wanted Jonathan to be her student, "because a child who wants music this badly should never be denied."

She took him in then. She took us both in. They would play together, and I would listen. He improved, dramatically. Not just his music, but his joy. Eve and I both realized, before long, that he was not just capable, he was fundamentally talented.

He had a soul that keened for the expression that he could not even hear.

I was making decent money by then. I was working in logistics, designing systems to enable trucking and train networks to interact efficiently. Nonetheless, I kept working for Jonathan. After my day job, I would go home and keep improving the tools he had for his music. I programmed a special pair of eyeglasses for him. They could show the patterns of the music on their lenses. With them, Jonathan could see what he was playing without needing a screen in front of him.

Eve kept pushing the envelope as well. She taught him to play with others, in duets with her. She taught him to 'hear' others play, not just himself. I helped with that. Using directional microphones, some pretty sweet processing software and some seriously fast hardware, I managed to cast his own music over one eye and the music of others over the other eye.

Jonathan learned to play in an ensemble.

We developed a special personality for him. He pretended to have Asperger's – just so he could avoid conversation. Such behavior wasn't unusual for prodigy. We wanted to hide his deafness so it wouldn't drown out his music. In a group, he would take instruction, but he would never ask questions. He was a mystery to others. Even his colored dancing glasses were left unexplained.

Then, one night, after a long day of practice, I put on one his father's recordings. I plugged it directly into the computer, it produced no sound. But Eve, Jonathan and I *watched* together. We watched the notes unfold. I cried, remembering what was lost. Eve comforted me. And Jonathan kept growing.

--

Now we are here. We are in a concert hall, filled with an expectant audience. And Eve and Jonathan, my wife and my adopted son, are about to perform Vivaldi's Cello Concerto in C Minor.

They are about to perform the piece that started it all.

As the bows touch the strings of the cellos, my eyes are closed.

And as the music unfolds, I hear the depth and meaning I have been seeking since Edgar's death.

But I hear more than that. As the music unfolds, I hear the soul of my brother. I hear his voice reaching out to me and telling me I have done what was needed.

I open my eyes and look at the stage.

Jonathan is there, swaying as he plays.

Remarkably, his eyes are closed.

Among other things, this week's Torah portion of BEHAR is about the land. It is about letting the land rest on its sabbatical. It is about paying for land based on its crops, with no discount for the risk that future crops might not be realized.

There are reasonable objections to these ideas. If we do not harvest on the seventh year, we will starve. If there is a flood or a frost, we will overpay for land that did not yield the fullness of its crops. Between now and YOVEL (Jubilee), we could die or be injured. In the *real* world, we discount for risk. We charge interest. We pay less for the crops expected in 10 years' time than we do for the food we can eat now.

We imagine we live in the real world, but our reality *can be* something else entirely. This is a concept core to Judaism: The world is full of risk and loss, but if we ignore it – if we resist it – if we embrace the timeless – then the nature of the world can be changed.

As Jonathan's story shows us, we *can,* through *EMUNAH* (belief) and the force of our wills, create a better reality.

The laws that surround our treatment of the timeless land (unlike the human-defined cities) reinforce this.

Lev. 25:20 *And if ye shall say: 'What shall we eat the seventh year? behold, we may not sow, nor gather in our increase';* ***21*** *then I will command My blessing upon you in the sixth year, and it shall bring forth produce for the three years.*

26:3 *If ye walk in My statutes, and keep My commandments, and do them;* ***4*** *then I will give your rains in their season, and the land shall yield her produce, and the trees of the field shall yield their fruit.*

Bechukotai: Duncan Jones

The voice is that of a young woman. She is beautiful, with a generally approachable smile that makes everybody who speaks to her feel welcome and appreciated; even as they know she's well outside their class. At this moment, her smile is more twisted. There's a hint of anger in it.

Actually, there's *more* than a hint of anger. The anger is raging inside her.

"We'll all just quit and see how long he can survive without us!" she declares.

The two of us, and twelve others, are standing in slacks, tailored shirts and custom shoes in a cornfield in Minnesota. A cornfield. None of us have bags or cell phones or any real possibility of hiding those sorts of things on our bodies. Our cars are a half-mile away. And, to add insult to injury, it is three in the morning and chilly. Not wintertime cold, we'd probably be dead in that case. But summertime chilly.

It is *not* comfortable.

A word wells up inside of me. And before I can stop myself, I find it spitting itself out, angrily.

"No," I announce.

Thirteen faces look in my direction. I see their surprised expressions in the clear moonlight.

"You want to keep working for the man?" asks the attractive young woman. She's surprised.

An older man, in his mid-50s, looks at me through his designer-brand eyeglasses, "Are you afraid he'll hurt us?"

The thought hadn't occurred to me. Then again, we are meeting in a field at 3AM to talk about a man who is halfway around the world in Central Africa. I guess it should have occurred to me.

"No, and no," I say. I answer the first question truthfully. But I lie, with necessary confidence, about the second.

"Then what?" asks another person.

I look around the little group, with their expectant, waiting faces.

"You're all alike," I say, "You all come from the same place and are doing the same thing."

I see confusion in their faces.

"How many of you imagined you'd be stealthily meeting in a damned cornfield, given our line of work?"

I see them glancing around, as if suddenly realizing how freakishly weird the whole thing is.

"We raise money for charity," I continue, "And we're damned good at it. In fact, I feel confident saying we're the very best there is."

Heads nod, proudly.

"But you didn't get good at this by being aggressive, ego-filled, people. You got good at this because, fundamentally, you like to help out those around you. You're good people."

There were more nods of approval.

"And we're listeners. We don't just listen to words and arguments. We hear what people *need* and we help them realize it. And so many people *need* a cause. So, you hitch yourselves to a cause, a worthy cause, and you help those people scratch that itch. We hear what they need, in their souls, and we give it to them."

More nods. But now, there is more than that. Some faces are furrowed in concentration. I get the impressions most of the people in this august gathering have never given that much thought to what they do. They aren't like me.

"We have a calling," I say, "And we are the best at that calling. But we only have so many years to make that calling real. Our careers might be 45 years long. We're at the peak of our skills for maybe 10 of those years. We have ten years to scratch our own itch. We have 10 years to truly live for a cause. That's it."

I pause, and then there's a whispered voice in the small crowd, "And Duncan Jones has taken 7 of mine."

"6 for me," says another.

The numbers flow around the small group, announcing themselves in hushed and mournful tones.

"He took five years from me," I say, "Five years I spent thinking he was changing the world. Five years I thought I was enabling a great man to accomplish great things."

It is no hyperbole.

Duncan Jones is a genius of charity. He'd gone to Central Africa, and he'd made a study, a real study, of the poverty there. He'd launched a whole series of initiatives to do what had never been done before: to actually fix things.

Where others had simply brought low-interest loans as a road out of the poverty trap, Duncan Jones had tapped into more fundamental human drives. Those who paid off loans in a timely manner were rewarded not with more loans, but with small luxuries – gifts of appreciation and self-reward. Chocolates were particularly effective.

Where others had pumped money into a corrupt economy, Duncan Jones had introduced his own scrip, his own currency. It was electronic, and you had to pass a personal audit to use it. When you did, you got a card that interfaced with the country's wireless network, so you could spend it anywhere. Duncan Jones stored people's money centrally, giving people who lived in constant fear of losing their personal possessions the confidence to actually save money and think about tomorrow. Of course, the scrip could be exchanged for local cash (or dollars) on request.

Where others dedicated resources to low-cost, high-impact, surgeries – surgeries that *did* change lives – Duncan Jones paired those surgeries with massive educational credits. That way, those who had been rescued, or their relatives, might eventually become surgeons themselves.

He not only gave hope, he gave purpose to the suddenly hopeful.

Duncan Jones realized the need to satisfy more than a balance sheet and his holistic vision seemed an unmitigated success.

That was why we raised money for him. He was the farmer, planting seeds of ideas – and we were the land, enabling them to flourish. We raised money, vast sums of money, to underwrite his incredible efforts.

It had all been going so well. Testimonials and smiling faces and cold hard numbers all reinforced this truth. He had targeted a vast rural area and it seemed to be flourishing.

The first sign that something was wrong had come in innocuously. One of our proud donors had gone down to visit the region. Duncan Jones didn't like those visits. He thought them patronizing. He thought, no matter how good their intentions that the happy white faces mixing with the happy black faces ended up sustaining a culture of dependency where none was ultimately needed.

He didn't mingle with the people.

But donors will be donors and they often prove hard to stop.

This donor, a sprightly older white woman from New York with the little glasses that speak of properly pseudo-intellectual values, strode into Duncan's world. She was impressed with what she saw. She was impressed, until the very last day, when she turned on the radio.

She'd funded a radio network in that same country. It hadn't been one of Duncan Jones' ideas. The purpose of the radio network was to broadcast market prices nationally so local growers wouldn't be taken advantage of by unscrupulous businessmen.

The problem was, when she tuned to the channel she'd paid for, all she heard was static.

She asked Duncan about it, and she wasn't satisfied with his answer.

She came home and asked her contact in our group, the older man with the fashionable glasses, about it. He responded by sending an agent to investigate. It was the agent who'd asked us to gather in the Minnesota cornfield.

The agent, the name he gave us was Mazi, was a tall black man with a huge forehead that seemed to be thrust out of his smaller, rounded, face. He seemed to use that massive forehead well. He was a very smart man, as demonstrated both by the complexity of what'd he'd uncovered and by the simple fact that he'd returned to tell us of it.

"Mr. Jones," Mazi had explained in his central African accent, "Is a clever man. He lifted incomes, just as he promised. But he only works in rural areas. Areas that have limited access to supplies and equipment."

"So?" asked one of the fundraisers in the group.

"So," said Mazi, "His efforts raise incomes. But he has cornered the markets for the regions he helps. And he has unofficial employees, knife-wielding street toughs from the capital, who create another economic reality. I've identified all his top lieutenants."

"What?" a shaky voice had asked.

Mazi explained, "If the farmers want seed, or a sickle, or bricks for a well – they must buy it from one of his proxies. He's run sham audits for them. They are all his people and their prices have been adjusted for the income of the community. It is all very advanced and tightly run. Which is why we're meeting in a cornfield. I have to assume he's monitoring you carefully."

"What does that mean?" asked a young man in the group. Obviously, he wasn't the brightest of the attendees.

"It means," said Mazi, "That every dollar you raise eventually makes its way into the pockets of Duncan Jones."

There'd been a collective gasp at that statement. Not everybody had understood the mechanism, but they understood the implications.

Mazi continued, "He's built himself a house on a hill with formal gardens and a statuary. He's built himself an army of men. He's built himself a small empire."

There was a whistle. And then the attractive and approachable young woman – her name is Amber – had announced, with moral certainty and satisfaction (and, yes, anger), "We'll all just quit and see how long he can survive without us."

That had been only moments ago.

I replied, "For five years I thought I was helping a great man change the world. I thought I was a good man, helping him. But I wasn't always a good man. I used to work for another leader. She didn't lie to me. She was a thief and a con-artist, and I was her enabler. We raised *huge* sums on the backs of her schemes. I lived for me."

The faces around me are stunned at this.

"We were never arrested or anything. My record is spotless. The money she stole vanished, looking like it had all been spent as it was supposed to have been. The donors were satisfied at the good they'd done. It seemed like there was no real harm – our victims bought real redemption with the money we stole – and they had the money to lose. Nonetheless, that work gnawed at my soul. And then, one day, I realized I'd had enough. And I'd done what Amber proposed just now. In a moral huff, I quit. And I found myself another leader, one I thought was worthy."

The faces are rapt now, drawn into my story.

"I had a few good years left and I spent them on Duncan Jones. I was scratching my own itch, my own need for a higher cause. And I was cheated. We were all cheated."

The heads nod again.

But then I'm hit with a rush of ideas.

"So," I say, "I am not going to just quit. Not again. I'm not going to be satisfied feeling all high and mighty and moral as I walk away from this mess. I'm going to, for the first time in my life, be the actor and the enabler of my own plans."

"What plans?" asks the older man with the stylish glasses.

"We're going to make an example of Mr. Jones." I say.

Various forms of assent ripple through the group.

"First," I say, "We'll fire a warning shot across his bow. He has played casually with the values we embrace. And so, we'll warn him. We'll cut off his money for a week."

Heads nod.

"But we won't quit. We'll leave him wondering where it has gone. We'll leave him worried somebody else is stealing it. And he might get the point. Mazi here will listen for the radio with the crop prices. If it comes back on, then we'll back off."

"But he won't turn the radio back on," I say with certainty, "The lack of radio is critical to his survival on the top of his layers of criminal underlings. No, he knows he can survive being cut off. He's created an actual economy. He's living off it. He can just spend a bit less, lower his prices a touch, but still gather his criminal proceeds. So, we won't warn him about the next step, or tell him about it even after we've done it. I have a friend from my old work. He can put a lock on Mr. Jones' passport. We'll seal him into the country."

I pause and look around. Some are already anticipating a delicious revenge.

"Of course,' I say, "That won't stop him either. No, he runs a criminal gang and rules the countryside. The only thing that will stop him is revolt by his own people. If the radio has still not returned, we'll 'accidently' send the next batch of money to the lieutenants Mazi has identified. Some will be loyal and report the money. But not all. Some will smell opportunity. They are cutthroats, not honorable men. And Mr. Jones will get a taste of what it's like when the culture of dependency – the culture dependent on him – is choked out and dies."

"What will happen?" asks Amber. Her voice is both frightened and somehow physically excited. I find it energizing. I feel my old persona coming back to the fore. I feel the thrill of a touch of destruction.

"Mr. Jones," I say, "Will be properly frightened. We'll break the pride of his power, and his enemies will rule over him. He will be consumed by terror. His soul will be harassed. His attempts to reap the profits of his lands will come to nothing. His lieutenants will fight and like beasts, they will overrun his estates and ruin them. He made a contract with us, and he will suffer for having broken it. His house will be burned, his statuary flattened, and he will flee in fear. The sound of a leaf in the wind will drive him from place to place. His white face will live in constant fear, trapped in the world of his enemies. He will never be able to blend in with those who hate him."

"And then?" asks Amber, her teeth biting into her lower lip.

I consider. We could drive him to death. But I found redemption, and so perhaps, so can he.

"He is a genius," I say, "A unique genius of charity. We still want to fulfill our potential and no man could do more than he to make it real."

They are just watching.

"Eventually," I continue, "When the cutthroats have burned through their money and his empire, they will be shocked at the devastation that has been left behind and they'll return to the capital. And, eventually, when we feel he has learned and suffered enough, we'll restore his money and enable his old lands to yield their human potential once again. Eventually, he will return. Not to serve himself, but to serve our mutual vision of the good."

"So, we won't quit," says Amber.

"No," I say, "This is our calling. He is a unique man. We will suffer with him, desolate and unsatisfied. Our only satisfaction will be knowing that no evil is being done in our name. But that will not be the end of our story."

I look around carefully, to emphasize my point, "Eventually, we will share in his complete redemption."

I feel my anger receding. There is hope and purpose within me once again.

Then, as the heads of the others begin to nod in agreement, we set about the business of reinventing an evil man.

This week's portion of *BEHAR-BECHUKOTAI* is about the land. Blood is *DAM* (דם). It represents potential, bringing life to our cells. Man is *ADAM* (אדם), the willful container of that potential. In the Garden of Eden, Adam is meant to plant crops in *ADAMA* (אדמה), the land.

The land, the feminine of 'man', is meant to actualize Adam's will just as the female womb is necessary to actualize the reproductive will of man.

In *BEHAR-BECHUKOTAI*, the land is betrayed, and it turns against the Jewish people. The people do not let it rest on its Sabbaths. They work it, for their profit, but do not let it serve its higher, *holy* purpose – which is ultimately the cycle of creation and rest with the timeless.

In this story, the fundraisers are the land. They are necessary to actualize the will of Duncan Jones. They yield their fruit. But they are betrayed. Their higher goal, the service to a greater cause, is denied.

In the Torah, the land, like the storyteller, once served another master. The land served Canaan and yielded great fruits (for example the massive cluster of grapes). But it cast off that corrupt service and sought something greater. It sought a farmer gifted with our enormous potential for holiness.

Having dedicated itself to holiness, the land is not satisfied simply expelling those who deny it its Sabbaths. It must make an example of them so that they can eventually return, ready and able to fulfill a mutual destiny.

The curses and ultimate blessings in the story are adapted from Lev 26: 16-44.

Pesach: The Gulf Exodus

The offices of the recruitment agency were gleaming. They were clean, modern and full of empty space. It was like no place I'd ever been in before. I felt safe. Now I know I shouldn't have.

I grew up on the edge of Mumbai Airport. We slept, ate, drank and worked in our little neighborhood. The airport runway, with its rumbling planes, was only 350 meters from my parent's shack. I could feel the planes landing, all day, every day, like they were next to my head. The rumble of their engines and squeal of their tires was the most regular part of my life. It was more regular than food itself.

The runway itself was three times as long as our neighborhood while the airport was 16 times the size of the 0.3 sq. km. we occupied. Over 30,000 people lived in our tiny space. From the perspective of the passengers in the planes, I imagined we looked like a collection of trash along the side of a road. We knew better, though. We were 30,000 people, with lives and stories and love and hope and sorrow. We were our own little world. We were never more than a few feet from each other. And the smells – skillets, sweat and sewage, all tinged with the spices of our land – were a constant in our lives. We were a bubbling mass of human reality.

I saw the airport every day. I *felt* the airport every day. But I could not go there. My clothing and the obvious poverty marked by it, kept me out. I never tried to go there. I belonged in what other people called a slum and I rarely left it. I belonged in my community. I stuck out from my people in only one way: I spoke English. My parents insisted that I learn it as they had. It was my only 'qualification' in the outside world.

I was fifteen when I fell in love with a boy. He was a handsome dreamer of a man. We had two children. And then he fell from the third story of a construction site and, after three hard days, died. Suddenly, I had two children and no way to feed them on my own.

I did what I could. I borrowed money. I did sewing and cooking and any other little bits of work I could find. But, slowly and surely, I was being dragged down. I could not recover. My only purpose was to be wrung dry by those who had loaned me money. When I had no more to give, it would all be over. The undertow of circumstance was going to destroy me and my children. I had seen it happen to so many others.

I was desperate when I heard about the man. He'd been travelling through the slum. He was looking for people like me. People who were willing to leave. And, most importantly, people who spoke English.

I went to the address he had shared. It was the address for the recruitment agency.

The agency had a gleaming, modern, *spacious* office. The guard at the door saw me and he *opened* the door for me. I was welcome in this place, not some reject from the lowest classes of society. I greeted him in English, and he greeted me.

There was an interview process. They tested my English, and they asked me about my domestic skills. I knew that not just anybody could apply. I knew I was special. It was reassuring. Once I passed those steps, they brought me to a computer. I had never used a computer before. I was suddenly worried. But then they called somebody on the computer. I was shocked when I saw a family in the computer. I talked to them, and they to me. They were different, but I could see the joy and open happiness on their faces and the faces of their children. They were a good family. And, they had a beautiful home. It was even nicer than the office. It was the final stage of my interview.

When the recruiter asked if I wanted the job, I considered his offer for only a moment. If this family needed somebody to wash their dishes and clean their house and cook their meals, I could be that person. I needed what they could offer. My children needed it.

I didn't have the $1,200 referral fee the employment agency required. I only had $126. So, I borrowed the remainder from the employment agency itself. I knew they would take the repayments from my salary. But that was actually reassuring. The agency wanted to be paid back, so they must believe my employers would honor their salary commitments.

The agency walked me through the process of applying for a passport. Then, before I left, they gave me a signing bonus. It was $100 USD. Half went to pay off my debt to them. And half, $50, went to me. I had enough to feed my children for over a month. I gave my mother the money.

The passport application was processed quickly. The next day, for the first time in my life, I entered the airport. The airport felt strange to me. It was so wide open, so dead. There was not only a lack of people; there was a lack of *my* people. It smelled faintly of cardamom, like some sterilized version of the India I knew. I felt quite scared. Nonetheless, I boarded one of those planes – the planes I had always felt roaring past our little shacks. I was shocked by the luxury within. I knew every rivet of every aircraft, from the outside. But I had never imagined what the insides were like.

As we took off, I looked down at my home. It looked like a pile of garbage, but I knew it was where I belonged.

I landed in Doha a little less than an hour later. The airport here was truly empty. My work visa was stamped by an officer in a booth. I noticed it named my employer, but I didn't recognize the name. As I walked out of the immigration hall, a man greeted me. He was the man I'd seen in the video. He introduced himself as Abdul. Abdul was smiling and warm. He smelled of a spice, but not something I was familiar with. It was something new. He had an Indian driver. Abdul and I sat in the back. He talked to me, greeting me and welcoming me to Qatar. I smiled back. I saw the Indian's eyes in the rearview mirror; but they had an emotion I couldn't understand.

A few minutes later, we arrived at a house. It was a creamy, two-story tall, concrete structure. There were windows, but they were covered with some sort of shade. When Abdul guided me out of the car, I realized, with sudden force, that there was no life in this place; I could smell only the barren dust of the desert.

Abdul didn't seem to notice. We walked up the stairs and the door opened. Behind it I saw a large and luxurious home. It was *like* the home I'd seen in the video, but not quite the same. I was confused. There was another man there. He was older than Abdul. And he did not seem friendly. He looked me over, lasciviously. The two men spoke and then Abdul, who I thought was my employer, simply passed me over to the other man.

When I crossed the threshold of that home, everything changed.

First, the man brought me to a crawlspace under the stairs. He mimed to me, gesturing at the space. I asked him, in English, what he wanted.

But he didn't speak English. That scared me even more. I had not been chosen for my only 'qualification.'

He mimed again, and I realized the space – a space without a door – was to be my room. It was smaller than the space I'd slept in in Mumbai; I would need to curl up to fit in it. And there was no bed or dresser, only a concrete floor. It was a stunning contrast to the rest of the house.

I left my few belongings there and then came back out, ready to work. I would make do.

The beatings started immediately. I was told to wash dishes. As I did, the mistress of the house struck me with a wooden spoon. She seemed to hate me, for a reason I could not understand. I was told to clean the living room. There, the man slapped me *hard* with his hand. Even the children, a boy and a girl no older than 12, hit me repeatedly. I wasn't sure what I was doing wrong, I wasn't sure I was doing anything wrong. But I resolved to get through it. I needed the money.

And then, that night, the master of the house – as I'd begun to think of him – attacked me in my closet of a room. That night, I decided I didn't really need the money. There was nothing I needed *that* badly.

I tried to leave in the morning, but the door was locked. I found a key and tried, once again, to leave. I was beaten, badly, for my efforts. The mistress seemed to take new pleasure in the beatings. I realized that she knew what had happened. It had not been my choice, but that did not matter. It wasn't me she was angry with.

When I saw the man, I said I'd go to the police. He understood that. But he laughed. Then, in one English sentence that sounded like it had been rehearsed, he said, "And they will cut off your head for adultery."

By the end of that second day, I was covered in welts. That night I broke a window. I escaped through it and ran until I found the police.

I was grateful to discover that they spoke English. But the gratitude didn't last long. I didn't tell them about the nighttime attacks, but I told them I wanted to leave. I told them about the beatings. But they just smiled at me, like I was some kind of childish idiot.

I showed them my passport. They took it and patiently explained to me what my visa *really* meant. I was part of the *kalafa* system. I was required to stay with my employer, for five years. I could not leave his home, much less the country, without his permission.

In the morning, the master entered the station. He complained about the broken window. They took notes, and then they returned me to him. I was taken back to his house and then I was beaten, far more severely than I'd ever been beaten before. Afterwards, I was barely able to walk but I was made to work for that entire day. Whenever I slowed, much less stopped, I was beaten. To make matters worse, I was not fed.

There was also no food the following day. I had no food and no drink. Gradually, I began to understand that I had no hope and no power. There was no escape.

It took a few more weeks for my hopes to disappear completely. I slowly came to withdraw from any choices or decisions. I could no longer help my children. I had no way of knowing if my salary was even being paid.

It took me a few weeks to stop crying. But I did. Then I saw myself in the mirror and discovered I had the same eyes as Abdul's Indian driver had had. I was no longer thinking. I was human in body alone. In every other way, I was simply an extension of my master. I did as I was commanded. I did not think, and I did not question my treatment, even to myself.

It just was as it was. There was no past and no future. There was only now and next, a next that was chosen for me. I was a slave. A slave confined to this home.

Only one hope remained. My contract ended after five years.

I longed for the outside world. I wanted to know how my children were, and how my parents were. But I could not get any news of them. My only connection to the world outside the home's walls was the TV in the living room. There was news there. But it was world news and seemed to have no bearing on my life.

Three years into my slavery I heard news of India. Tremendous oil reserves had been discovered off the western coast. They called it "Underwater Shale." I didn't understand the importance, not right away. But, over the coming years, I heard about my country's growing wealth. The newfound resources, combined with a tremendous simplification of the regulatory state, led to massive growth. I heard about slums being replaced by proper apartment buildings and of the lower-caste masses being lifted from their poverty. I heard of an unprecedented economic miracle. None of it mattered. I could have hoped that my children had survived to see the times of prosperity. But I would not allow myself to do so. The pain was too great. Only when my five years were complete would I allow myself to be human again.

As I entered my fifth year, I began to count down the remaining days of my slavery. There would be an end to this. There would be freedom. My body was covered in scars. I felt hollowed out. But there would be freedom. When the five years were up, I walked to the front door, expecting to be released. It was all that I had. But my master, in the Arabic language I had learned, just laughed.

He showed me a statement. He explained that it was my balance. My debt to the employment agency had grown to over $4000. I had been paid only a fraction of what I had been promised and the interest on my debt had approached 50% per year. In addition, I still owed him for the window. He showed me a new visa. And a new contract. He had signed it on my behalf. I was, he explained, *never* going to leave.

His son, five years older than the day I had arrived, came to me that night.

For the first time in years, I cried. I did not cry for rescue; I knew that would not come. I cried because any remaining hope had been quashed. There was to be nothing left of me. I had almost forgotten my name.

The next day, I saw on the news that the Indian Navy had parked a fleet off the Persian Gulf. They demanded that their citizens, be allowed to visit their families. They insisted that they, the great Indian nation, would set the rules from this point forward. Two weeks of leave must be permitted, they said, and then we could return to work.

I was stunned by this news. But it offered no hope. I knew what would happen. I was not surprised when my master beat me more vigorously than he had before. Then they added to my work. They had bought flour before, but now they bought only wheat berries. They required *me* to grind the flour for the family.

My muscles ached. The pain was so bad I could not, even in my limited way, think. All I knew is that I wanted my countrymen to leave; they were causing me pain that I did not need.

The attacks started the next day. I could feel the shockwave from the oilfield that the Indian air force destroyed. It represented the heart of this nation, I knew. But the Qataris did not back down. Next were government buildings and roads and power stations. I felt the world around me closing in. My master and his family listened to a hand cranked radio now. The station was Jordanian. But the Qataris were not giving in. They were masters of the universe. I knew I was not worth this suffering. My labor was not worth this cost. But the pride of the Qataris, the pride of these masters who saw me as nothing, was too great to accept defeat.

Gradually, though, even I began to realize redemption was at hand.

One day, with the lights out, the pantry empty and the house stinking because of plumbing failures, I heard a booming voice. It didn't come from the radio. It came from the air and from the sea. And it commanded us, the domestics and the laborers, to drive to the sea and to sail to our freedom.

I felt pride, pride in my people. Pride in India.

I broke my second window that night. And then, together with over ten thousand others, we streamed to the sea. Our masters were too frightened to stop us.

Of course, many did not leave. Somehow, Qatar had become their home.

The rest of us boarded the dhows and pushed off illuminated by the moon. Only then did we discover there was no oil in the little ship's tanks. They had been drained in the course of the emergency. None of us were used to thinking ahead. We still had the minds of slaves. But we pressed on, using our hands then, to paddle out to the waiting navy.

The Qataris were not done yet though. They sailed out after us, armed with their navies and their pride. We feared them. We could not outrun them.

But then, a wall of fire appeared before us. It took us a long moment to realize it was the guns on the decks of the Indian ships.

In a moment of fury, it was all over.

In a moment, we were free.

When I returned to India, I found my children living with my parents in a block of apartments our community had built near our original neighborhood. It smelled like home. Like many others from my neighborhood, I found a real job, with a real salary.

Today, I am working at the newly expanded airport.

We are free now. But we were slaves. And so, every year my fellow *Kalafa* workers and I celebrate our redemption.

For five days, one for each year of our slavery, we abstain from petroleum. We abstain from that which had made our former masters great.

And on the sixth day we use that same petroleum to light a wall of flame, celebrating the power it has given our people.

The Global Slavery Index ranks Israel the 48th worst nation for slavery with 11,600 estimated slaves. There are an estimated 3 million slaves in the Middle East and North Africa. Their conditions are often worse than those described in the story. I wrote this story to try and capture some of the feelings of surrendering to slavery. The story of redemption parallels that described in the Book of Shemot/Exodus.

Pesach: Mulualem

My phone buzzes again. It's maybe the tenth time in the last hour. I pull it out of my pocket and glance at its shattered screen. It is my father, again. He probably wants me to come home.

I slide the phone back into my pocket, unanswered.

There's no moon tonight and so the street is even darker than usual. A low glow from the mega-city that is the Israeli coast hovers in the air. But it only allows vague shapes to be seen. There is no definition. At least not in the darkness. Of course, the whole street isn't cast in that indiscriminate darkness. Stained concrete buildings, worn-down public housing, are set back from the road and the light. They have harsh-looking plazas in front of them, lit by the yellow glow of sodium lamps. During the day, parents sit on the broken benches while their children play between the weeds. During the night, teenagers hang out there, ensconced in the safety of the lights.

There are also streetlamps set between the plazas. They are spaced far from one another. Young Kushi[1] men, men like me, hang out below them. The lights serve as a sort of sign. An advertisement. They say: you can find trouble here.

My phone buzzes again. I don't bother to pull it out of my pocket. I just let it vibrate against my leg. I'm beginning to regret even having it. I thought it'd be nice, but it's beginning to annoy me.

I watch an ambulance zoom by its lights flashing in the darkness. Maybe one of the paramedics is like me, a Kushi struggling at the bottom of his own world. But even as that imaginary Kushi drives by, I realize that I am below even him. I'm a street cleaner. I work from

---

[1] This is a highly racist term – I'm using it intentionally, *not* with disregard to its implications.

dawn 'til dusk in some fancy town full of rich white people. They barely even see me. I'm just a yellow jacket picking their trash off the sidewalk in the mornings. That said, there are benefits to the work. Today, I found the phone outside an apartment block. Somebody had bought it once. They'd spent good money on it. And then it was shattered, and abandoned, and left out as trash.

When I picked it up, it was almost like finding an old friend.

The people who threw it away didn't clear its memory. I guessed their lock pattern, a simple U. I opened it and I found pictures, hundreds of pictures. Of another world. Of children playing in perfect parks. Of restaurants. Of large apartments with designer furniture, sparkling homes and expensive art hanging on the walls.

The phone is a window into another world. But not mine.

My world is humid and hot and smells of damp concrete.

As the cars drive past, I feel their white lights passing over us. I imagine their drivers peering into the cones of light cast by their cars. I imagine them seeing the dark forms along the side of the road. And I know what those drivers are feeling as they see us. I see it during the day. Some are angry, although I can't imagine why. Some feel pity, which I understand. But most? Most feel fear.

They are frightened of us.

Even Kushi drivers are frightened of us. Sometimes, just because I can, I glare at the passing cars. I have little power, but I still have the power to frighten the privileged with only a look.

A car pulls to a stop. I accept cash and deliver drugs. The man in the car is a regular customer. The streetlamps are my signpost. They announce that I'm open for business. But I don't need a streetlamp. The way I figure it, I could be wearing a suit and tie and people would still think I'm a drug dealer. They'll never look up to me. I'm a Kushi. So why shouldn't I do what they already expect of me?

I belong here on the street. I fit. It may not be an exalted reality, but at least I fit. There's some comfort in that.

My phone buzzes again.

It's my father, again.

My father doesn't fit. My father refuses to fit.

My father had been a big man back in Ethiopia. He'd been respected. He'd been important. And then he made the most fateful decision of his life. He decided to come here. He came here, a helpless black savage stuffed into the back of an airplane. A black savage hoping to find the Messiah. And that's what he's remained. A helpless black savage. An uneducated and illiterate man. A monkey in a modern world. And yet, somehow, he still hopes to find his Messiah. Even as the world squeezes him into his proper place, he refuses to accept it. He refuses to accept what he really is. He hopes somebody will eventually realize he's deserving of their respect. But the more he demands respect, the less the world gives it to him. Even my mother divorced him. She was ready to move on. She left us all.

Still, he reaches for the past. He doesn't seem to understand that the past is gone. I hate him for it.

He calls again.

This time, I pick up?

"What?" I ask, letting the anger into my voice.

"Why haven you answered your phone?" he demands.

I consider lying, pretending my 'new' phone wasn't working. But I don't care enough. I don't say anything.

"Come home, now!" says my father.

"Why?" I ask, trying to draw out the word as a sort of antidote to his impatience.

"The elevator was broken. Your ayati tried to take the stairs." My ayati, my grandmother, is named Nikahywot.

"And?"

"Mulualem," my father says, "Your ayati fell. The ambulance is here now. I need you to come home."

"Okay," I say, reluctantly. I end the call, walk out of the light of the streetlamp, and head home.

My ayati isn't like my father. She came here, physically. But she never left Ethiopia. In Israel, she is only a frail, lost, useless woman. She can do nothing. She's never tried to fix that. She is only here because we are. And even that link is tenuous. She speaks Amharic, as does my father. But my sister and I don't. Like so many of our generation, we speak only Hebrew with a smattering of Arabic. So, she moves around her ever dwindling community of elderly Ethiopians. She watches her children and her children's children. She watches, but she understands nothing. She's not a part of our world.

When I get to our building just a few minutes later, the ambulance is still there. But the strobes on top of it are off. Just then, I know what's happened.

My ayeti is dead.

I slowly walk up the poorly lit staircase. Dark mold peers out from between the peeling pink paint on the walls. All of it is highlighted by the unnatural shine of the cheap fluorescent lights. Level after level I climb, expecting to find my grandmother around the next turn. But there is nothing.

Then, one story below my home, I come across the paramedics. And I come across my ayeti. She is laid out on a stretcher and covered by a sheet. The paramedics are just waiting now, for the coroner to arrive. My father is standing next to them. He's crying. But I imagine, in a day or two, he'll barely notice that the old woman is gone.

She was just a shadow.

I slip past my father. He looks at me, begging me for something. But I don't know what. I head into the apartment. I pull a bag of cheap bread out of the cupboard and some hummus from the refrigerator. I start to eat. A minute later, my father comes in.

"You have to help me?" he says.

"With what?" I ask.

"Maybe they'll have forms," he says. My father can speak Hebrew reasonably well. But he can't read it. He likes to have me around when forms need to be filled out.

"And if you fill them wrong? Does that make ayati more dead?" I ask.

He glowers at me. He wants something from me. Maybe comfort. Maybe support. He hasn't earned that, though. I just look at him, as I absentmindedly chew my sandwich. I'm insulting him with my eyes, and we both know it.

A moment later, he turns and walks from the room.

Just then, I get an idea. I shove my sandwich in my mouth and pop up from my chair. I've heard of old grandmothers sewing gold into their clothes. Maybe my ayati had something valuable in her room. My father will be busy with the coroner for at least a little while. This is my chance.

I step into her room and quietly close the door. I flick on the overhead light – a bulb hanging from exposed wires. Then I begin to dig.

It doesn't take me long to find what I want.

In the closet I find a small, ancient-looking, wooden box. I open it and inside I see a small clay figurine. It is clearly a lion, but it looks like a child's conception of a lion. It has a rough, rounded shape and it is painted in bright colors. Its whole body is surrounded by a thin iron exo-skeleton. What looks like hammered threads of iron run up the insides and outsides of the legs, merging along the belly and the the back – giving a sharp contrast to the softness of the clay.

I close the box and slip out of the room, taking it with me.

The next morning, I'm up early. My ayeti has been taken away by the *Chevra Kadisha*, the burial society. Her funeral will be in the afternoon. Which leaves me the morning. As my father sits in our tiny living room, I slip out of the house – the small box hidden in my bag. There are art galleries on the other side of the town, the side with gleaming white towers. One of them, I know, specializes in Ethiopian art.

Thirty minutes later, I walk in the door of the gallery. There's a saleswoman there. She's dressed in an elegant and perfectly tailored suit. She looks up at me. I can see the suspicion almost immediately. It is an Ethiopian gallery, but Kushi don't often come here.

"I want to sell something." I say.

Her comprehension and relief are obvious.

"What," she asks.

I pull the box from my bag and open it on the countertop. The saleswoman's eyes go wide.

"It is my grandmother's," I say, "She gave it to me. She said it was hundreds of years old. She said it was a lion of Judah"

"Why are you selling it?" asks the woman, staring at the little clay and iron lion.

"I don't want to," I lie, "We just need the money."

The woman doesn't even touch the piece, she just looks at it, examining it from every angle.

"Again, I have to ask, are you sure you want to sell this?" she asks.

"I must," I say, "That's why I'm here."

Who would have thought selling something would be so hard.

She looks up at me, assessing my expression.

"Do you have any idea what this is worth?"

I want to say yes, so she won't cheat me. But I really have no idea.

"To you," she says, "It should be priceless."

"Everything has a price."

She nods wistfully. "Do you have any paperwork, showing you own it?"

"Paperwork? Why would there be paperwork. She gave it to me."

The woman nods, knowingly. Ethiopians aren't famous for paperwork.

"This is an old piece," she says, "I don't know how old. But it is very valuable. I'm sure it has been in your family for a very very long time. You really shouldn't sell it."

How much convincing will this woman need?

"I need to," I say, "My grandmother needs medical care in America. But we don't have the money. She gave it to me to sell."

The woman's face shifts to pity, a familiar expression. People act most predictably when they think you are being the most predictable.

"Okay," she says, "But I still think you should think very carefully about this."

She thinks for a moment longer, "Listen, I'll sell it on commission. If you come back before it sells, you can take it back. If not, then I'll take 5% of its sales price when it sells."

"How much will that be?" I ask.

"I don't know," she says, "But it ought to be worth more than 10,000 shekels."

"Wow," I think to myself.

I shake my head to mask my excitement.

"I only wish I didn't need to do it," I say.

She nods, knowingly. Although, of course, she knows nothing. Then she pulls a form out from under the counter. She jots in the details of our agreement. We both sign it and then, carefully, delicately, she closes the box.

She looks up at me, "I hope your grandmother has a complete recovery."

"I hope so too," I say. A minute later, I leave the gallery.

10,000 shekels is a lot of money.

A few hours later, my ayati is buried. There is a single Kess (or Ethiopian-Jewish cleric) there, shaded by colorful umbrella and wrapped in his finest white robes. My father speaks briefly. He talks about their voyage together. About my ayati's desire to be here. About her desire for her children to be here. Then he pauses, uncertain. I know what he's thinking. She desired it, but her children did not. It was all a mistake. He doesn't share that thought, though. Instead, his voice just peters away into silence.

The Kess steps forward then. He states, as if it is fact, that my ayati must be full of joy now. After a hundred generations, she is blessed by not only seeing – but being buried in – the Land of Israel. It is a nice thought, but I hardly think she has an opinion on the matter.

The funeral is short, the attendance sparse. Before long, we go home. I imagine that our lives will continue, just as before. After all, my ayati was never really here.

But my father has other ideas. He goes into her room. And then, a few minutes later, he emerges. He was sad at the funeral, but now he is distraught.

"It's missing," he says.

My sister and I just stare at him. "What?" I ask.

"The lion," he says.

"What lion?!?" my sister asks. Unlike me, she really has no idea what he's talking about.

"The lion of Judah is missing," my father says again. His eyes turn to me, and I can see they are flashing with anger.

"You took it!" he shouts at me. "Tell me where it is you *assama!*"

"WHAT?" I shout back, "What 'lion' are you talking about?"

My father tears past me and shoots into the room my sister and I share. I hear drawers being thrown open. My sister looks at me, but I just shrug.

10,000 shekels is a lot of money.

A few minutes later my father emerges from the room. His eyes are full of fury.

"Where the hell is it?" he shouts at me.

"Where the hell is WHAT?" I shout back.

He glowers at me. And then he charges back into my ayati's room. He tears through her things, tossing them to the sides as he violently searches for the little clay lion.

"Aba," I say, trying to sound calming, "What are you looking for?"

"A lion," he says, "A little clay lion wrapped in iron."

"Why is it so important?" I ask.

"It just is," he snaps.

My sister and I stand in the hallway as my father rips through the apartment searching everything but finding nothing. After all, there is nothing to find. He searches everything 3 times, and then 4. Eventually, reluctantly, he begins to slow. Like an engine that has run out of gas, he gradually comes to a stop. And then, collapsing on the living room chair, puts his heads in his hands. And he just sits.

"Aba?" I ask.

He looks up briefly. There is resignation in his every move.

"It's gone," he says.

"It's just a statue," I say.

He looks at me, shocked at my lack of comprehension. And then his eyes dim in front of me.

In that instant, I realize that everything is gone. The fight that had defined him is gone. The resistance to reality that had kept him together has vanished. And in that moment, I know that 10,000 shekels is a lot of money. I also know that it isn't enough.

I may hate my father, but even I can't rip out his soul.

My sister and I help my father to bed. And then I slip out of the house again. Within 30 minutes, I'm back at the art gallery. I step inside. The same saleswoman is there. Her face is pitying, but also seems to offer some kind comfort.

"We sold it," she says.

She gives a hint of a smile. "In one day, we sold it for 15,000 shekels."

I just stare at her.

"But I don't want to sell it."

She looks shocked. "But your grandmother…"

"She died," I say. "A heart attack. This afternoon. The funeral is tomorrow."

The saleswoman stares at me.

"Who was the buyer?" I say, "Maybe I can explain and get it back?"

"Some Americans," she says, "They paid in cash. I have no idea who they were."

"Where were they staying?" I ask.

"I don't know."

"What did they look like?"

"Ashkenazi," she says, referring to European Jews.

"Do you have video?" I ask.

She does. And she shares it. I use my phone, trying to find the faces online. I find nothing, though. I print a copy of the faces. I visit the local hotels. But I find nothing.

The buyers, and the lion, are nowhere to be found.

I go back to the gallery and the saleswomen hands me my 14,400 shekels.

14,400 shekels. Apparently, the price of my father's soul.

--

When I get home, my father is still in his room. Visitors come, to speak about my ayeti. But he stays in his room, getting up to greet no one. My sisters offers to cut his hair, as is our mourning tradition. But he refuses. When she brings him food, he only picks at it. Days pass. Only when it is time to go to work again does he leave his room. He is a different man, though. His eyes are sunken. His expression is dead. He isn't even angry at me.

Weeks pass like this, his lifeless form moving in and out of the house. Slowly, I come to realize what I have to do. I have to recreate the Lion of Judah.

There's an art supply store in the mall. I go there, looking for guidance, and looking for clay. Another saleswoman helps me. She asks if I have a kiln. I say no. She recommends some oven-baked synthetic clay. But I know that would never work. Instead, I buy clay – real clay. I'll find a kiln when I need one.

I don't go home. I can't let my father know that I took the lion. If he sees me trying to recreate it, he will *know* my ignorance was feigned. Instead, I go to another neighborhood. Not Ethiopian, but Yemenite. There's a small park there. I sit on a park bench set before a park table. Then I set to work, forming and shaping the clay. But the material slips through my fingers, it refuses to mold to my touch. It grabs onto the dirt and grime that surrounds me. It rejects every effort I make. It will not be shaped.

I can't seem to make anything, much less a child-like lion of Judah. I can't stop, though. Day after day, I come here after my work. I pour himself into making this single simple piece. A lion of Judah. Day after day, I work to the point of exhaustion. I show up to work so tired that my boss thinks I'm on drugs. He doesn't test me, because he doesn't *really* care. He *expects* me to be on drugs. Despite it all, I make no progress. It is like the clay is fighting *me*.

It is like the clay is refusing *my* attempts to atone for my sins.

One night, I'm sitting on that bench. I've bought batch after batch of clay, and I've ruined them all. I've achieved nothing. I am achieving nothing. It is so late that even the dogs have gone to sleep. I'm so tired that my thoughts seem to drift and merge and slip easily into the realm of nonsense.

I can achieve nothing. And, yet, I have to keep trying.

And that is when I hear the voice.

"Mulualem," it says, calling me by my name. It is the voice of a woman. Her voice is soft and vaguely familiar.

I just sit there, not understanding *where* the voice is coming from.

"Mulualem," she says, "I can help you."

I can hear her words roll off her tongue. They are smooth, comforting, beautiful – like stones being gently worn away by a river's water. I realize, in surprise, that she's speaking in a language I've only heard the Kessim speak. She's speaking Geez.

And I understand her.

"Help me, please," I say. Somehow, the same language comes from within me, the ancient language of my people.

"Throw out your clay," she says. I do as she says.

"What now?" I ask.

"You need to find your own clay," she says.

"Where?" I ask.

"Where there is fresh water and soil, mixing together."

I begin to walk then. I feel as if a hand is holding mine. Guiding me forward in the night. It leads me to a place I would not have expected. In my neighborhood, behind my building, surrounded by the smell of trash and a floating cloud of insects, there is a pipe.

It collects the water from the air conditioners in the building. It deposits that water here, behind the building.

The mud here is thick beneath my feet.

The place is disgusting. But her voice reassures me.

"This is the place."

And then I feel her hands again. They guide mine into the mud. I feel as my fingers are submerged into the goop.

"You feel that?" she asks. I do. I can feel the mud, and it seems to wrap around my fingers – embracing them.

"Pull it out," she says. And I do.

The mud is there, in my hands.

"Roll it in your fingers."

I do. I feel it taking shape in my hands.

"Wrap it around your fingers."

I do. And I feel it curve smoothly around them.

"Shape it into a ball."

I do as she says. The material comes away from my fingers.

"Yes," says the voice, "This is the place."

There's a discarded bucket there. As she commands me, I gather more mud from the hole. I collect it in the bucket.

"What now?" I ask.

But instead of answering, I see the process in front of me. I must dry the clay, then crush it and soak it until it has the consistency of heavy cream. Then I will pour the top of the thin slurry out and through a screen. When it has settled, I will pour out the extra water, remove the clay, smooth it out and let it dry.

Only then, when it is nearly dry enough, is it ready to be worked.

"Purification," she says, "It is a process of purification. Only when the clay is pure is it ready to be worked."

I feel it then, in my hands. I know what it must feel like when it is ready.

"What then?" I ask.

But the voice is no longer there.

Over the next three days, I do as I was told. I dry and soak and process and purify the material. But when I try to work it, I can't. I can't form it. It cracks between my fingers. It doesn't feel as it did in my vision. It isn't quite ready to be fashioned.

I take the clay, again. And I process it again. Drying and soaking and purifying. And again, I fail. And again, I try. Cycle after cycle, I try. With each cycle the clay comes closer to what I felt in my vision.

Month after month passes. Summer passes to winter. And then winter to spring.

And then I finally I know it is ready. I *know* I can form it. But when I try to shape it, it resists me. It refuses my efforts. It does not allow itself to be formed.

It is rejecting *me,* and I don't know why.

I wrap the clay in plastic bags, saving it.

I do not know what else to do.

Pesach – Passover – is coming and I feel no closer to bringing life back to my father.

Pesach is as it always is, only smaller. The three of us sit together at our small table. Hard European Matzot adorn the center of the table. Eventually we reach the meal, and my father explains, *again*, how his family used to smash their plates before Pesach and fire new ones, fresh for the festival. He has told us this story every year. There was excitement in his voice, once. There was joy in the telling. But every year, I ignored him. This year his voice is dead. He seems to be growing even more listless. This year there is no joy. Only this year, I am paying attention.

"Do you remember *how* you did it?" I ask. My father ignores me.

"Do you remember *why* you did it?" He doesn't answer.

"Why won't you answer?" I demand.

It is then that my father places his tired hands on the table. He turns to me, his eyes almost soulless. And he says, "You don't deserve an answer."

Before long he has left the table. I mourn as I watch him go. He's vanishing from the world, and I've chased him from it.

I go to bed, but I can't sleep. And so, in the middle of night, I get up. I leave the apartment. I go to the bins in the back, to my hidden stash of perfect clay. The place is even more disgusting than usual – the refuse of Pesach cleaning piled up in the bins. The insects seem to fill the air, but I ignore them.

Instead, I just stare at the clay. My need to shape it has reached deep within me. Every part of me, every cell in my body, is focused on that clay. I am willing to sit forever, until somehow it takes shape before me. So, I sit there, hour after hour – somehow hoping to form it with my mind.

Eventually, I nod off.

Only then do I hear the voice again.

"Mulualem," she says. That musical, familiar, voice speaks out; somehow overcoming the smell of the collected garbage.

"Yes," I answer, snapping to attention. The Geez flows off my tongue.

"Now you are ready."

I feel the hands again. They guide me to the clay. And then, as I begin to work the material, I feel it finally move – as it should – beneath my fingers. It flows around my fingers, obeying them. The voice speaks to me: "It isn't the surface of the clay that gives it its form. The life of the clay is beneath, buried in the heart of the material. You have to feel that and work *out* from that. Only then can you give it life. But it takes time. It can't happen all at once. You have to build a foundation and then work from there."

I look down at my hands and I see what I have formed. There is a simple plate there. It is rough and unadorned. But I have given it form.

I look at it, amazed at my achievement. And then I hear the voice speaking to me once again. "In Ethiopia, those who could change the form of a thing were called *buda*. They were cursed because only the cursed would engage in such witchcraft. We Jews were *buda*. We were forced to work with iron and clay. It set us apart."

"Am I cursed?" I ask.

But the voice doesn't answer. Instead, it simply says, "I will return when you are ready."

"Ready for what?" I ask.

But there is no answer.

The presence is gone.

I come back the next night. The plate is dry and ready to be fired. But I don't know how to fire it. I can find a kiln, but I know that's not what's meant to be. I could look up directions online, but I know they will not work. Without the presence, I cannot work the material. Without the presence, I won't be able to fire it. That is not the path I must be following.

The voice will return when I am ready.

I return to the clay. Day after day, week after week. I destroy and rewet and reform. I learn, step by step. I form plates and then bowls and then pots. I form simple sculptures. Bit by bit, remembering the feel of her hands, I learn to work the material. I learn to work from it from its heart.

I get better and better at my craft.

All the while, my father is growing weaker.

Then he summons us, his two children, to the table. And he tells us, listlessly, that he has been diagnosed with cancer – and that he cannot be cured.

He has only weeks to live and he seems not to care.

I work even more furiously. Hour after hour, day after day, I try to craft the lion. But I can't. And even if I could, I could never learn to work the iron before my father's time has passed.

And then one night, as my father sleeps in his bed, fitful and weak, I see what I must do.

I cannot form the lion. The lion will not be mine. But I can form something else.

My hands grasp the material and I shape it between them. It flows beautifully in hands. And with my hands, I build a man with a square heart. Lines, below the surface and above it, stream out of it to every part of his body. They start as strong ridges in the clay, but they get thinner and thinner. I see it and as it comes to me, I shape it in the clay. The lines seem fluid, changing and yet completely permanent. There is life in them. There is life in *him*.

I know that, once it is dry, the presence will return.

When I come back the next night, she is waiting for me. Once again, she shows me what I must do. Together we build a firepit with kindling and bricks. She shows me how, as the kindling burns, the object will tumble into the fire. She shows me how to protect it from that fall – so it does not shatter. She shows me how the intense fire will set it. Then, she shows me how to capture the smoke so that the object will emerge with a treasured shade of black.

I work as she speaks. Hours later, the object emerges.

It is a small figure. It is charcoal black. And it is beautiful.

When it cools, I begin to paint it – driven by an image in my mind. I write a word in Geez upon it: "Torah." I paint the heart with a strong gold color. Then I paint thin lines over the ridges that lead from its heart. The painted lines grow thicker and stronger even as the ridges slowly fade away.

And then the little figurine is done.

The vision is gone, but I don't need it. Not anymore.

I have formed a man from clay and and blown the spirit of G-d into it. I hold it in my hand, and I realize what it is.

It is my people.

The heart of my people is our Torah. But it flows from our distant past, our history, and it spreads within us – somehow growing stronger even as our spoken words – the paint - overwhelm those that are written – the ridges.

But the truth runs deeper than the form and the colors. Like the little figure, we are drawn from a place of rejection, of ultimate exile. We are purified and recast again and again. Only *we* can be recast, again and again. Because our oral Torah and our history were never captured and fixed and hardened by being set in books, we have kept our malleability and its life. Our words, person to person, generation to generation, shape a deeper and richer reality. And so, again and again, through our persecution, we have been molded from our very core. We have been molded by the challenges of our exile. We have been molded. And now we are ready.

Now we are here. In Israel. The fire has been lit. And I know that we are ready to come to life. We are ready to take on our ultimate form.

But we must rest just right in the fire. Otherwise, as we tumble into the core of it, we will shatter. All of our history will be lost, and our form will be cast aside.

I take the little figure in my hands. I carry it, the representation of my people, to my father. He opens his tired eyes.

He sees the little figurine. And in that moment, for the first time since my ayati died, I see life and light in his eyes.

"Who taught you?" he asks. Suddenly I know. Suddenly, I recognize the voice that guided me. It was the voice of my Ayeti. Nikahywot.

"Ayati," I say.

"Ayati," he smiles. "Nikahywot."

Then he translates her name, although I know what it means.

"She is the source of life."

As he lays there, I ask what I had asked at the seder: "Why did we smash the plates before Pesach?"

My father smiles. "That is the wrong question, Mulualem. The question is: why do we *fashion* plates for Pesach?"

"Why?" I ask.

He asks me to sit him up in his bed. And then he says, "Mulualem, we smash our plates to avoid eating the slightest crumb left on them. This is because Egypt was the source of bread. We didn't belong there."

He pauses to catch his breath. I just wait for him to continue. And then he does. "Mulualem, the Ethiopians rejected *buda* – the making of new forms. So, we also smashed our plates so we *could make new ones*. So, we could reject Ethiopia. Because we didn't belong there either."

After another break, he continues, "But it isn't enough just to leave a place. We *need* to remember we were in Egypt. And we *need* to remember we were in Ethiopia. Because we can only find our future through our past."

He squeezes my hand and then smiles, once more.

I sit then, with my father.

I sit with him for three days. And then the cancer takes him.

--

Three years have passed. I am still a street cleaner. I still collect trash from the sidewalks of a rich Ashkenazi town. I still see the eyes of others as they look at me. Some are angry. Some pity me. Most remain frightened of me. But they do not understand. They do not know that my people are tumbling into the fire. They do not know that we are being crafted by G-d. But I know. And I know we must land gently – or else we will crack and be destroyed.

So, when my workday comes to an end, I take the bus to a small river. Dozens of children, the children of my people, are waiting there for me. Together, we will dig for clay and will I tell them the story of our people.

Together, we will make dishes for Pesach.

My people have the power of *buda*.

We can change our form; even if others never see past the color of our skin.

Author's Note

The Biblical Joseph was given *useful* interpretations when he gave credit to Hashem for his understanding. He finally gave full credit to G-d when he said:

בלעדי: אלקים יענה

"It is not in me, G-d will answer."

I am not a scholar. Instead, I often finding myself asking Hashem for an answer to difficult questions. Almost invariably, a little while later, I find the answer I need, and it becomes a part of what I share and what I write.

I don't think this is anything unusual. I believe *all of us* can do this. We just have to be open to asking, and then be ready to listen to the answers we are given.

Joseph Cox lives in Modiin, Israel and is blessed with a wonderful wife and six children. If this book added to your life, do someone else a favor and share it. Also, *please please* add a review online. It makes an enormous difference.

That's me!

Other Books by the Author

Adult Fiction

The City on the Heights (a novel)

Candidate Everyone

The Hidden Agent

The Boulevard, Torah Shorts Volume 2

The Assessors, Torah Shorts Volume 3

Pete and the Felon, Torah Shorts Volume 4

The Barn, Torah Shorts Volume 5

Children's Fiction

Grobar and the Mind Control Potion

Squiggles and the Pit of Destruction

Autobiography

A Multi Colored Coat

www.ingramcontent.com/pod-product-compliance
Lightning Source LLC
Chambersburg PA
CBHW021924170626
46807CB00007B/2977